The Boys
and the
Bees

The Boys
and the
Bees

Joe Babcock

CARROLL & GRAF PUBLISHERS
NEW YORK

THE BOYS AND THE BEES

Carroll & Graf Publishers
An Imprint of Avalon Publishing Group Inc.
245 West 17th Street
11th Floor
New York, NY 10011

AVALON
publishing group incorporated

First Carroll & Graf edition 2006

Library of Congress Cataloging-in-Publication Data is available.

ISBN-10: 0-7867-1647-9
ISBN-13: 978-0-78671-647-0

Printed in the United States of America
Interior design by Maria Elias
Distributed by Publishers Group West

This book is dedicated to my father,
who has always loved me and
accepted me for being gay.

Chapter 1

S itting in my dad's recliner with the TV on, I listened to my mom gather up her purse and keys as her heels clicked across the kitchen floor. Dad ran downstairs then back up. Probably forgot his wallet. I changed the channel to a sitcom about teenage daughters. I hoped this episode had a kiss. It was the summer before sixth grade.

My parents came into the living room. Dad wore a brassy brown beard and glasses. Mom wore her dark chocolate hair shoulder length, a red shirt, and jeans. They were on a dart league at the Mermaid Bowling

Alley, which they no longer took me to, since I was eleven and old enough to babysit my sister, Amy, who was only six.

"I'm sure Amy will be in bed on her own in half an hour," Mom said, "but I don't want you staying up past midnight."

"Be good," Dad added.

With that, the garage door opened and the deadbolt snapped. Seconds later, their car crawled down the gravel driveway. I hopped onto the couch, leaning over the back of it and peeking behind the drapes. The car pulled onto Otis Avenue then zoomed off into the night.

A family of raccoons crossed the street toward the neighbors' house. My dad hated raccoons because they were vandals. I felt bad for them. They lived by the Mississippi River, which was only two blocks away from my house. There were a few stars in the sky. Finding the brightest one, I wished sixth grade to be my best year ever.

I leapt back onto my dad's recliner and grabbed the remote control. I was not allowed to watch HBO, but I broke that rule and found an R-rated action movie. Biting my nails and turning down the volume so Amy wouldn't hear, I hoped to see nudity. I ate a Symphony bar and microwave French fries, drank Cherry Coke, and pecked away at my typewriter, which was perched on a TV tray.

I was writing my third novel. Twenty-two pages and counting. So far my protagonist, Beverly, had run away from home to escape her abusive stepdad, finding a haven at her uncle Buford's deserted cabin in the woods. There, she fished, gardened vegetables, and made friends with a fox named Craig, a bluebird named Wobblygums, and three squirrels, which were yet unnamed. I'd decided to make it interesting, so on page seventeen Beverly finds a picture of a cute boy underneath a tree and, disregarding the protests of her animal friends, goes into town to find him.

I decided to name the boy Mark. Mark Saddle was my best friend's name, and the picture Beverly finds is actually Mark's cute yearbook photo from last year. Beverly and Mark were going to fall in love and live happily ever after!

BANG! BANG! BANG! rapped the doorknocker. Someone was at my front door! With lightning-fast reflex I grabbed the remote and changed the channel. After that I was too scared to move an inch. BANG! BANG! BANG! The knocker pounded. A man's voice shouted, "Anybody home?"

I gasped silently. I couldn't move. What if he was a murderer?

"Hello?"

He knew I was home. I crawled on my hands and knees to the door and called out. "Who's there?"

"Hello?" the man shouted. "Is it all right if I use your phone? My car died."

Oh no! I didn't know what to do! I couldn't be rude. What if that upset him further? I opened the door slowly to see a man with a pierced nose and left eyebrow. I was about to scream—

The man lunged at me and grabbed my shoulders. "Hey, kid, don't scream. I'm not here to hurt you." He stepped back onto the porch with his hands up. "See, you can slam the door on me. I'll just go to the next house."

I stared at his black hair, which looked like a Mohawk and was probably dyed since he also sported an upside-down triangle of brown hair on his chin, and surveyed his black leather jacket with steel studs. He looked like a criminal. He arched his pointy eyebrows and smirked. "Are your parents home?"

"They're sleeping," I said.

He put his hand on the door to hold it open. "Look, my ma's car broke down. Is it okay if I use your phone?"

"Wait here," I said, running to the kitchen to get the cordless.

When I returned, the stranger hadn't moved. Fleetingly, I wondered if I should wait inside the house while he made his call on the front porch, but then I wondered if he'd steal the phone, so I crept out onto the porch and closed the door behind me.

"Nice phone," he said. "Mind if I smoke?" He put a cigarette in his mouth.

"No," I said, figuring that it was sure to be all

right, since my parents let their friends smoke even inside the house.

The stranger lit his cigarette with a match and began to punch at the buttons on the phone. "What?" he asked. "You want a drag?"

"Um . . . yeah . . . sure," I said, trying to sound cool.

The stranger had the phone to his ear, waiting for an answer, his eyes intent on me as I reached for the cigarette. When he handed it off to me, I felt a surge of tingles, as if it were a wand. I took a drag, coughing my head off instantly and dropping the cigarette.

As tears streamed down my face, the stranger began to speak. "Paul, my ma's car broke down. . . . Yeah, I know. Piece of junk. . . . Can you pick me up? I'm on Otis, down by River Road. Some kid let me use his phone. . . . Yeah, I'll just wait by the car. . . . Thanks, Paul. You're a doll. . . . I love you," the stranger said playfully.

He noticed my surprise and grinned wickedly. "Thanks, kid. You're a good Samaritan." He handed me the phone then picked the cigarette up and put it out on the sole of his black boot. "You can keep this," he said. I thought the offering was strange and possibly an insult but I didn't say anything but "Thanks."

The screen door shut behind him, and I watched him head to his car. I returned to the house and locked the door, then leaned up against it, eyeing the cigarette butt in my palm. I was still frazzled. And dizzy.

I trudged up the stairs laughing hysterically. That

was so weird! I never thought I'd actually try a cigarette! My bedroom was a big mess. In bed I thought about the stranger. I didn't know his name, but I knew Paul's name. I thought about that and fell asleep.

* * *

The next morning I woke up groggy. When I went downstairs for breakfast, my parents immediately said they wanted to have a talk with me. They only teamed up on my sister or me when we were in huge trouble. I reluctantly sat down with them at the dining room table. They sent Amy to her bedroom. Then Dad set the cigarette butt down on the center of the table. I remembered my crazy dream. I'd been underwater and feeling all sexy.

"We found *this* last night on the landing," Dad said, thrusting his finger at the cigarette butt.

I was speechless and couldn't believe what a moron I was for dropping the stupid thing on the landing.

Mom jumped in. "You're eleven years old!"

"Where did you get this? School?" Dad asked.

"Um. . . . No."

"Where then?"

"I found it. . . . on River Road."

"Why on earth did you pick it up?" Mom demanded.

"I don't know. . . ."

"Damn those motherless corporations and their candy cigarettes!" Dad howled. He looked straight at me. "I don't ever want to see you smoking."

"What were you thinking, Andy?" Mom asked.

"I wasn't thinking. Sorry."

"Well, think!" Dad said. Then his face slackened. He'd gotten the word across sufficiently, and to make it stick he sent me to my room.

I sat in my room and thought about what serious trouble I was in. I'd smoked a cigarette and I was only eleven years old! If any of the kids at school knew, they'd freak. Cigarettes were for dropouts and criminals. Again, I wondered if the stranger was a criminal. I swept my hand across my chest, making the sign of the cross.

Looking out the window at treetops, I wondered what had become of the stranger. He had said, "I love you" to Paul. Who was Paul? Maybe they were brothers. I imagined the two of them in an apartment or something, wrestling. I buried my face in my pillow. They would kick my ass if they knew what I was thinking. I prayed not to grow up weird. Something deep inside told me I was never going to be the same.

Chapter 2

When I was six years old, my dad took me down to the Mississippi River for the first time. The river divided Minneapolis and St. Paul. We lived two blocks away from it, on the St. Paul side. To get to the river's edge we had to walk down about a million steps, because the hills on both sides of the river were covered with trees and in some spots rocky cliffs. Dad and I had been walking along the riverbank when suddenly he sprinted off the path and climbed one of the cliffs like a giant bug. I was stunned. I couldn't believe my own dad could pull off such an amazing feat. I knew I couldn't have done it. Maybe someday I'd try.

Earlier this summer I thought it would be fun to take my friend James Bugler down to the river on the St. Paul side. James was a real girl about getting dirty and I wanted to gross him out, so I didn't tell him about the stairs and made him climb down the treacherous hill with me. We had to go on our hands and knees, clinging to branches so as not to tumble down. James yelled at me all the way down about how I was always getting us into trouble and how one of these days we were going to get hurt. James was such a cry-baby! Even for an eleven-year-old.

When we finally made it down, we sat at the river's edge. James's face was red from the excursion. I suggested he take off his shirt to cool down. He said he would if I would. So we both took off our shirts. James and I were both skinny. I liked the way we looked together.

One night during a sleepover James asked me what was so special about the river's edge. I told him that for hundreds of years there'd been murders, gang wars, and pagan psychos doing rituals down by the river, adding that sometimes kids still disappeared. James's blue eyes went cross. He didn't believe me at all. So I elaborated all night long. Finally James started crying and said he hated me, because I got him to admit that if my story weren't true, maybe a lot of the other things he believed in, like God, weren't true either.

* * *

On the morning of my first day of sixth grade, I wouldn't get out of the bathroom until my hair was perfect and my cowlick pressed down. Finally, Mom had to yell at me because I was going to miss my bus. I was so excited when I entered my new homeroom. I had Sister Mary Kelly, everyone's favorite teacher at St. Mark's. She was one of those fat, jolly people who jiggled like Jell-O when she laughed.

The other sixth-grade teacher, Mrs. Lorenz, was mean. I had her for math. Everyone in Mrs. Lorenz's class wished they were in our class.

All the kids stopped what they were doing when Sister Mary Kelly entered the classroom, sat at her desk, and proceeded to dig into her three-gallon black purse, pulling out a TV remote. She looked from it to the class then burst into laughter. She said that somehow she had mistaken it for her keys and that Mr. Preston, the principal, had had to let her into the building. How Sister Mary Kelly could have mistaken a remote control for keys was beyond me!

The first thing Sister Mary Kelly did was assign us to our desks. We sat boy, girl, boy, girl. I sat between Molly Purdy and Alexandria Marsh. Everyone moaned about it, including me, even though I loved the arrangement. Molly and Alexandria were pretty girls, and I just knew we'd have a blast passing notes together.

To my supreme satisfaction, Mark Saddle sat in front of me, which meant that I could stare at the back of his handsome head all day. Mark was blond like James, only he didn't look at all like a pretty girl. In my mind he was the most beautiful boy ever—like what I wished James and I looked like together—and he could probably pass for fourteen.

Mark was my best friend (he just didn't know it yet), and my goal was to play with him every recess. The new "in" game was football.

Our class had to go to church together sometimes, like on holidays or the first day of school. I made sure to sit next to Mark in the pew. Mark was friends with all the cool guys, and most of the time they hated me, unless I was being funny. The guys only liked me if I could make them laugh.

Brett Michaels, who was the shortest kid in our grade but popular nevertheless, dared me to pull Casey Fisher's hair. She was sitting in the pew in front of us, with her long brown hair hanging over the back of it. I wanted the guys to like me, so I did it without even thinking about Casey's feelings.

Casey screamed so loud that Father Frank skipped a beat in his sermon. "Andy Bobsees pulled my hair!" she shouted.

The whole school laughed their heads off, and I was suddenly so embarrassed that I couldn't even believe this was happening to me.

Mr. Preston dragged me out of church and into his office, where he yelled at me. "I'm surprised at you, Andy. You've always been such a nice boy. What on earth possessed you to pull Casey's hair? That was very cruel."

"I don't know." I didn't want to get Brett in trouble, because that would make me the biggest nerd, so I didn't tell Mr. Preston that I'd been acting on a dare.

"I don't want to see you turn into a troublemaker. You'll have to be reprimanded."

Thankfully, Mr. Preston didn't call my parents. Instead, he gave me detention for a month, which meant eating lunch at a table for one in the center of the crowded lunchroom and missing recess.

When I told James about my punishment, he was extremely alarmed. "How can you let Brett get away with it?" he bellowed.

I screwed up my eyes. "Unlike you, I stand up for people."

Like always, James looked at me as if I'd punched him in the stomach. I ran away.

Later that afternoon, I was about to get on the bus when Mark stopped me to ask what had happened in Mr. Preston's office. I told him about the detentions, and he felt terrible. "Brett should confess," Mark said. "He put you up to it. Want me to talk to him about it?"

"Oh . . . that's okay," I said. I was so embarrassed that I could not look Mark in the eyes. If I did, I'd start picturing him without his clothes on and imagine what it would be like to have a sleepover with him. He would think I was totally weird and tell everyone at school to hate me.

"You're a cool guy, Andy," Mark said. "You're not like the other guys."

I was astounded but tried not to let it show. "Really?"

"For sure. Catch ya later." Mark headed for his bike. I got on the bus, sat close to the window, and watched him pedal away.

* * *

The next day Beverly decided to go to town again. She took her blue dress down from the clothesline and fed Craig and his friends nuts and berries from her apron. Before she left for town, she ate another can of creamed corn. She was beginning to worry about food for the winter.

She skipped along the trail and tripped over a rock, falling on her knees. "Oh dear me, oh my!" she said when she saw an oozing red patch on each knee. She wished she'd brought some Band-Aids with her from home. She tore a piece off her dress and tied a scrap around each knee.

"Now all my dresses are ruined!" she thought sadly. Time to learn to sew!

When she got to the town, she went to the fountain in the center and looked to see if there were any coins. She was delighted to see the floor scattered with pennies and nickels. She reached her hand into the pool but halted to cough when a cloud of smoke blew into her face. She looked up to see a scary stranger with steel studs on his black leather jacket. He put on a pair of red plastic devil horns and grinned.

"Is it Halloween?" Beverly asked.

The stranger looked at her as though he didn't speak any English. "Hey, little girl, want some of this cigarette?" he rasped.

"You *do* speak English!" Beverly cried.

The stranger held out the cigarette and Beverly reached for it daintily. She took a drag and blew smoke rings. "Now I really must be on my way," she said, "I need to collect these coins to buy food."

"You mustn't steal other people's wishes," the stranger said.

"You're not my dad!"

"Little fool! Don't you know that stealing wishes will curse you?"

"How?"

"Not everyone makes good wishes." His eyes turned evil. "Some wishes are carnal!"

With fire in her eyes, Beverly ran away, into the

forest, to her uncle Buford's cabin. When she got there she went straight to bed.

* * *

I never would have pulled Casey Fisher's hair if I had known how humiliating detention was going to be. At lunchtime I had to sit in the center of the cafeteria, where everyone could see me. The entire school knew what I had done, and pretty soon opinions about what I had done were divided between the guys, who thought my existence was pathetic, and the girls, who hated me for being a hair-puller. I could hear their whispers behind my back as I ate my hot chicken sandwich.

James was sitting alone at the end of the fourth-grade table, which made it appear as though he was being punished, too. Having me for his only friend was what made both of us geeks. I had to do something to save our reputations. I remembered a trick that once made Amy shoot milk out of her nose at McDonald's. When the coast was clear of teachers, I dipped a pickle slice into ketchup and flung it at the wall below the clock, where it make a red smear and stuck. The entire room burst into laughter.

Mrs. Pringles, the gym teacher, who was on lunch duty, blew her whistle and scanned the room to see what was so funny, her gaze missing the pickle. When she looked away, I tossed another pickle and it stuck again, looking like a second green, bloody dot on the wall. Every kid in the lunchroom went into hysterics.

"Ouch!" I screamed at a pinch behind my arm.

"What do you think you're doing?" Mrs. Pringles spat, as she lifted me to my feet and escorted me out of the cafeteria to a deafening silence.

She took me to the principal's office and explained to Mr. Preston what I had done. Mr. Preston was livid. He said that apparently I craved a lot of attention this year, and that from now on I'd get attention—from him. Furthermore, I was going to spend the rest of my one-month detention serving hot lunch to the entire school, then washing dishes during recess.

This was horrible! I racked my brain all the way back to class. There had to be a way out of this mess.

* * *

I hoped Mark would be waiting for me at my bus again after school, but instead I found James standing in his place.

"What happened?" James asked.

"I don't want to talk about it."

"Do you want to go down to the river?"

I eyed James skeptically. "Sure."

I ditched my bus and we walked to the river. Trying to be careful not to dirty the school uniforms we were wearing, we climbed down the steep hill on our hands and knees. James slipped once or twice and freaked out because his mom was going to see all the mud. I told him he could wear one of my uniforms home.

"She'll notice," James said, out of breath and clinging to some tree roots.

"Who cares," I said, reaching for the next tree and swinging down a branch to the bottom. James followed, and we went to the edge of the river. James jumped at every strange noise. It was only when we weren't in class that I found James's timidity adorable. I just knew he could be so cute, if only he weren't such a girl. I put my arm around his shoulder and told him about a crazed serial killer, who reporters said had been stalking the river.

That night we had a sleepover.

Chapter 3

Sometimes I hated James. He was *such* a sissy. When Sister Mary Kelly had handed back our spelling tests that morning, he nearly cried because he'd misspelled "raspberry." I'd misspelled "ra*SP*berry," too—half the class had—but James almost had a nervous breakdown. He wasn't happy until Sister Mary Kelly said he could retake the test.

Kevin Timkey whispered to me, "What a faggot."

I was so angry with James for being a faggot that I ignored him for the rest of the morning. At church that afternoon, I prayed. I was embarrassed to tell God my darkest secret, so at first I beat around the bush and thanked Him for my parents, my writing talent, for my sister, and for Jesus. Then, with a feeling of flames all around me, I said, for the first time out loud in my head, "Please, God, don't make me be a faggot."

Earnestly I prayed for a wife and children one day. But I saw another future in my imaginary photo album. Me alone in a dingy one-room apartment, writing novels and getting gay movies in unmarked packages in the mail, which is what my cousin Vicki told me gay people did. Her uncle, who was only related to me by marriage, was gay, but no one in the family ever talked to him.

"Fix me," I prayed.

When mass ended, the teachers decided to let us have a ten-minute break because it was such fine weather. I joined Mark and all the guys on the front steps of the church. "Hey, guys," I said.

Mark said, "Hey, Andy." Everyone else ignored me.

"Man, Mr. Preston's passing out detentions like candy this year," Mark griped. "Did you guys hear about Nancy? She got detention just for talking too loud."

Kevin snickered. "Dude, I saw Nancy's panties today when she uncrossed her legs in math class. They got hearts and shit on 'em."

"No shit?" Brett said, all interested.

"Dude, who *hasn't* seen Nancy's panties?" Mathew Brenner chuckled. "She's got 'ho' written on 'em."

All the guys except for Mark pealed in laughter. "You shouldn't talk that way about girls," Mark berated them.

Brett rolled his eyes but didn't argue. Everyone obeyed Mark, because Mark was the leader of our group and always seemed to have good morals. I wanted to make him like me so bad. I had to say something cool. "I think girls are pretty," I said.

Mark smiled at me in surprise.

"*You* think girls are pretty?" Kevin asked. All the guys laughed.

"What?" I said. Isn't that what I was *supposed* to be thinking?

"Hey, Andy, why don't you go find James?" Brett asked. "He's wetting his pants over his spelling test."

They burst into laughter.

"Fuck you," I said.

"Or what?"

Brett was five inches shorter than me. Even though he acted tough, I knew he was scared of a real fight. Getting into his face, I said, "You think I won't kick your ass?"

Brett shuddered and I felt a surge of confidence.

"I don't want to fight you, man."

"Why? Are you scared?" I asked.

"No—I don't fight faggots," he said.

"*Oooh!*" all the guys screamed, now wailing with laughter.

Kevin practically gave me a noogie, pointing his finger in my face and shouting, "*Diiiiiiissss!* Diss on you!"

"Get off me," I said, pushing him off. "I'm not a faggot."

"Yes, you are," Brett said.

"No, I'm not."

"Yes, you are. I can tell."

I was staring Brett in the eyes, trying not to back down, wondering frantically how he could tell. What did he see? Did everyone see it? Did I look like a faggot right now? I was suddenly so disgusted with my body and face that I just wanted to crawl out of the world and be bodiless in the afterlife.

"Admit you're a faggot right now!" Brett insisted.

I almost said that I was. But Mark broke it up. "Lay off, guys, okay? I mean . . . he's not a faggot."

Brett leered at Mark skeptically. Mark seemed embarrassed too, and Brett knew it. "Yeah, whatever," he smirked.

Mark's face was beet red. Everyone in the circle was horribly uncomfortable, and it was all my fault! I had embarrassed Mark the same way James had embarrassed me so many times. Evidently, being a faggot was like having cooties, and if anyone tried to touch you, even to help you out, they caught the disease.

"Hi, guys," James said meekly, as he tried to join the group.

I tried not to show my surprise, even though I was

mortified to think of what James might say, since every time he opened his mouth he lisped. It was like being trapped in a nightmare! Mark would hate me after this.

The guys eyed James. Mark didn't look at him, and neither did I.

"Did I miss something?" James asked.

"Hey, James, how do spell 'raspberry'?"

"How do you spell 'moron'?" James retorted, and for some reason, that was the funniest thing that happened all day, and everyone, especially Mark, laughed.

* * *

Now that we were in sixth grade, everyone wanted to hang out after school. Usually we went to the triangle, where the guys played football and the girls watched. James never wanted to go, because he refused to play football. I also hated football but, unlike James, wasn't prepared to sacrifice the best years of my life over it.

I usually took the bus home after school, then changed out of my uniform and biked to the triangle. I pedaled as fast as I could through the red and yellow leaves that were falling from the trees. When the triangle popped into view, I spotted some of the guys playing catch. Mark wasn't among them, although I couldn't tell who all was there because of the hill.

I slowed down to watch for a moment, a feeling of dread in my stomach. I wondered if I should have just stayed home and worked on my novel instead. I thought about how my character Beverly wasn't good at sports. She could *only* do everything else. I wished I had an uncle's cabin to run to.

I remembered thinking on my first day of sixth grade that this was going to be the best year ever. But having Sister Mary Kelly for a homeroom teacher wasn't enough. For my wish to come true I needed to make people believe I wasn't a faggot.

At the triangle I dropped my bike beside all the other bikes on the grass and then ran down the hill and across the field. "Pass it here!" I shouted, waving my arms.

Mathew saw me and threw the football ahead of me so that I would meet it running. The ball was right there—an easy catch. Unfortunately, when I tried to clasp it to my chest, it bounced off my face and I fell over backward. I could hear the guffaws coming from the guys and imagined in horror how comical that must have looked. Scrambling around on the grass, I located the ball and jumped to my feet.

"Here!" Mark shouted, running toward me.

I did my quarterback stance—making like I was targeting him, then threw the ball. It arched perfectly but was off the mark, and Mark had to run backward and dive for it with some sort of exquisite cartwheel. He landed with his arms raised and the saved ball in one hand.

The guys cheered.

Kevin said, "That was some fuckin' air, dude!"

"That was some fuckin' Wang Lee moves—Wha-ya!" Mathew said, making Kung Fu stances.

Everyone gathered in the center of the field. We talked about Mark being a pro football player, but Mark said he was a baller, and we talked about basketball and how our team was going to kick ass this year. We were going to go all the way to the championships for the first time since our fathers were kids. Kevin brought up the subject of how I threw pickles at the wall in lunch.

"Dude," Mathew said, "that was so fucking funny the way those pickles stuck to the wall! I thought I would piss my pants!"

"What the fuck did Mr. Preston say?" Brett asked.

I said, "The fuckin' faggot is making me eat lunch with him."

They all laughed. "Dude, Mr. Preston is a total faggot."

"He's as a big a faggot as James!" Mathew said.

"Yeah," I said.

Brett smiled pleasantly. "I was wrong about you, Andy. We're cool."

I noticed Mark not paying attention anymore. I wondered if he was mad at me about something. Meanwhile, Brett was waiting for a response. "Yeah, man," I said, giving him a high five.

A few minutes later the girls showed up at the triangle wearing sweaters and toting a picnic basket.

Anna, the most popular girl in our grade, had gotten all the others to meet at her house with sandwiches. Some of the guys rolled their eyes at the "sissy" gesture. But as soon as they saw the food, their stomachs took over and they hungrily wolfed it down. None of the girls ate. I honestly wasn't hungry either. On the contrary, seeing the smiling faces of my gorgeous classmates filled me with joy. In junior high next year we'd all be signing yearbooks and going to dances and hanging out at the mall!

As soon as all the sandwiches had been devoured, the guys ran out to the field, tossing the football. I didn't go with them.

"Andy, boys are supposed to play football," Nancy told me.

"I have a sprained ankle," I said.

"Sure."

Anna grimaced at me. "You know you're evil for pulling Casey Fisher's hair in church."

"It was an accident."

Anna rolled her eyes.

God, I wished I were Anna. She was the only girl at our whole school who took ballet lessons, and she had a blond bob, luscious eyelashes, and heart-shaped lips. She was kind of flat-chested, and sometimes when we played volleyball in gym class she looked kind of sexy, like how James looked sexy because he looked like a girl. Not that I'd want to touch Anna's gross body! Barf! I wondered if someday the thought of naked girls wouldn't make me sick. Everyone said it would happen. But I didn't want it to happen. I thought about James. James was much cuter than any girl. Maybe I'd get him to sleep over tonight.

"Nancy, you're a lesbo. Why don't you play football?" Katy suggested.

"Lick my armpit," Nancy said.

"What's a lesbo?" Stacy asked.

Katy giggled. "A girl who likes girls."

"What do you mean?"

"What do you think she means?" Anna asked testily.

"I don't know."

"She means when two girls have sex," Nancy said.

"Eew," cried Stacy and Molly, who evidently were both learning something new.

"Why don't you girls start practicing?" Nancy suggested, as she stroked her own long brunette hair.

Stacy and Molly stared at each other as if they'd rather lick a toilet seat.

Nancy sighed. "Come on you guys, we're here to watch the boys."

I thought about the word "lesbo," which seemed to be the opposite of "faggot." I didn't think Nancy was really a lesbo. Already twice this year Mr. Preston had made the girls kneel so he could measure the distance from the hem of their skirts to the floor. It was supposed to be two inches. Most of the girls' hems were four to six inches, but Nancy's was an astonishing twelve inches. She'd gotten detention both times, yet she still sat in Mrs. Lorenz's math class crossing and uncrossing her legs, which is exactly what I would do if I were a girl, and I was definitely the opposite of a lesbo.

"I think Brett is cute," Nancy said, as she put on lipstick to the reflection in her compact. "I'm going to get him to make out with me."

"Oh my God, Nancy!" Anna exclaimed.

"What?" Nancy asked. "Aren't *you* going to kiss a boy this year? *Hello?* Aren't we *all* going to kiss the boys this year?"

I pondered the question deeply, gazing out at the field. The guys were in the middle of their game. One or two of them actually glanced our way.

"Kevin's right. You are a ho," Katy said.

Nancy scoffed. "Like I care what he thinks."

"Anna," Katy said sneakily, "Mark told me a secret."

All the girls, including me, stared at Katy like she had just blown sparks out of her ears.

"What's the secret?" Anna asked.

"He likes you. Like, a lot."

"Are you serious?" Anna squealed.

How could this be happening? Mark liked *Anna?!* Was it a joke? I'd never heard Mark talking about Anna before. Mark never talked about girls. And I loved that about Mark!

All the girls were giggling.

"Mark is so dreamy—go for him, Anna," Stacy said.

"You two will make the cutest couple," Katy added.

"I think I'm going to cry!" Alexandria cried.

Anna declared beamingly into the eyes of each and every friend. "This is going to be the best year ever!"

Chapter 4

That night Beverly stood at her sink, mildly surprised by what had happened that day. She recalled the stranger by the fountain with a shudder and what he'd said about stolen wishes coming true. She thought about all the coins she'd stolen from the fountain and half expected to find a stash of gold in the cupboard, or to become a princess. She wondered what kinds of evil wishes people made and shook with fear.

"I'm a bad girl," she reproached herself.

"Everyone thinks so," Wobblygums agreed, pecking birdseeds out of the windowsill.

"Well, I don't care what everyone thinks! I don't have time to worry about curses when I must find the boy in the picture!"

She sat by the hearth and warmed her toes. She wondered what she'd do when she found the boy in the picture.

Kiss him, of course!

* * *

I went downstairs to find Dad and Amy watching TV, while Mom read a book on the loveseat. She put her book down the moment she saw me and asked me to sit next to her. "You've been upstairs typing for a good hour. I take it your novel is coming along?"

"It's good," I replied nervously. "Beverly is looking for the boy in the picture."

"What's going to happen when she finds him?"

I blushed. "I don't know. . . ."

"Let me know when I can read it. Have you been keeping up with your homework?"

"Yes," I said, even though I had been scrambling to finish assignments ever since the beginning of the year. There were some assignments I never even turned in, and I lied about how many books I read. Sister Mary Kelly wasn't that strict.

"How is school going otherwise?"

"Fine. I'm best friends with Mark Saddle this year."

Mom eyed me skeptically. "What about being best friends with James?"

"Um . . . I dunno . . . James and I just don't have anything in common."

* * *

That weekend, Mom and Dad had their dart league, and as usual Amy and I were staying home alone. Mom had been too busy doing paperwork to make dinner, so they ordered a pizza for Amy and me. Mom said they wouldn't leave until the pizza arrived, because she didn't want me to answer the door when they weren't home. I argued that I was eleven years old and could order pizza by myself.

"Don't question your mother," Dad scolded.

It was so unfair.

"Can James at least sleep over?" I begged.

"Last night you said you and James didn't have anything in common," Mom reminded me.

I had forgotten I'd said that. But I didn't want to be alone tonight. "*Pleeeeease?*"

"All right," she finally agreed. "But only if it's okay with his parents—and don't make James hound them, like you usually do."

"I won't, I promise."

When the pizza arrived, Dad paid for the delivery guy, and Amy and I took the pizza into the living room and sat on the floor in front of the TV. Amy's favorite show was *Full House*, and watching it was torture. The moment Mom and Dad finally left, I changed the channel.

"Hey, you can't do that!" Amy cried. "Mom said I could watch it!"

"This is better." I flipped to *A Current Affair*. Amy sulked.

"You're supposed to use a plate! Mom said!" she screamed.

"Don't worry about me. Just eat your pizza."

"No! Mom said!"

"You want to play poker?"

Her eyes lit up delightedly. Amy loved poker. She'd learned how to count by winning pennies from Dad, and now her arithmetic skills belied her six years. "Can we play right now?"

"As soon as I call James."

She protruded her bottom lip at me.

"Hang on, I'm calling right now." I sat in Dad's recliner and dialed James's number.

"Oh, hi," James answered, trying to sound casual, even though I knew he was excited that I was calling, because he had no other friends.

"What are you doing?"

"Drawing."

I pictured James in his attic bedroom, lying in bed and drawing Teenage Mutant Ninja Turtles, which for some reason James was obsessed with drawing, and wearing shorts with an oversized red or turquoise Fruit-of-the-Loom T-shirt. He'd be wearing socks, of course. James only took off his socks when he was bathing or when I made him take them off during sleepovers. James had really cute feet, and one time I had sucked his toes.

"You want to sleep over tonight?" I asked.

"I can't."

"Why not?"

"Because my parents won't let me."

"But you always sleep over."

"That's why they won't let me. Besides, it's late."

"No, it's not. My parents went out to play darts. We can watch *Aliens*."

"Really?"

"Yeah."

"My parents will never let me."

"Can you ask them?"

I could detect a scowl in his voice. "*Fine.*"

A couple minutes later he came back. "They said no."

"What did you say?"

"I asked if I could sleep over."

"Ask again. Tell them it's really important."

"Why is it so important?"

"Because you've been reading all day and you need a break—to watch a PG movie with your friend," I added sarcastically.

"*Aliens* is rated R. One of these days my dad's going to find out."

"Impossible!"

"This conversation is impossible."

"No, it's not. I swear it's possible. Just ask them. Beg them. I begged my mom."

"Why do you want me to stay over so bad?" James asked, even though I was quite sure we both knew the answer. I wanted to try sucking his toes again—and more.

"Come on, please? Just beg them."

James scowled into the phone again. "*Fine.*"

A few minutes later he returned. "They said no again."

"What did you say?"

"I said what you said."

"*Ugh.* Come on. They have to let you. What? Are they going to keep you locked in that attic during the most important years of your life? Just explain how much you want to come here. They'll understand."

"No they won't."

"Tell your dad you'll rake the yard."

"*Fine!*" James said sullenly.

A few minutes later he asked, "My dad wants to know if your parents are home?"

"Well, duh, tell them yes."

"I can't lie."

"Come on! What's the big deal?"

He groaned. "Hang on."

When he returned he asked, "My dad wants to know if he has to drive?"

"Just ride your bike."

"They won't let me ride my bike in the dark."

"But it's not even dark."

"It's almost dark."

"Well, tell your dad that my dad's in the bathtub."

"What about your mom?"

"She's sick."

"They won't let me come over if she's sick."

"She's on a long distance phone call then."

"How can she be, when you're on the phone?"

"*Duh,* she has to make a long distance call as soon as I get off the phone."

"All right. Hold on."

James's dad finally agreed to drop him off at my house, and when he arrived we played poker with Amy on the living room floor. Amy and I had pennies and nickels to play with. James had to borrow. He already owed Amy $3.42, and she was practically a gangster. I figured he'd have to pay her someday. James didn't even like poker, but I had already promised Amy we'd play.

When Amy went to bed, we turned off all the lights and watched the movie. If my parents came home while it was on it was no big deal, because *Aliens* was one of the few R-rated movies I was allowed to watch.

I had to pause the movie when my parents came home and turned on all the lights. Mom chatted with

James and asked about all his brothers and sisters and parents, and James talked about how he'd been drawing lots of pictures of Teenage Mutant Ninja Turtles lately and blah, blah, blah, blah, blah. Finally, Mom and Dad went upstairs to bed, and James and I settled in to return to the movie.

After it ended we went to our fort in the basement. It was two old couches pressed together, covered by a makeshift canopy. We always played games and ate junk food in there. When we had crawled beneath the canopy and lay on our backs, I told James about the stranger, keeping to myself the part about Paul.

"I can't believe you opened the door! That was stupid!" James said.

"What's the big deal? He was cool. He let me take a drag off his cigarette."

"*What?*" James cried. "You smoked?"

"Yup."

"I don't believe you."

"It's true."

"You're lying."

"Fine. Don't believe me, *asshole.* But it's true."

We were both silent for a while.

"Why do you call me names?" James asked.

"Sorry," I said, even though I wasn't. I had something else planned.

I put my hand on James's thigh. He didn't respond, so I started sliding my hand around. I felt dirty doing it—

like I couldn't control myself from sinning. But I knew I'd never be able to fall asleep if we didn't play this game.

"I wish you didn't have detention every day," James said, like it was truly upsetting him.

"Mr. Preston is a faggot."

"What does that make us?"

I let go of James's thigh. "*Nothing.*"

We lay in silence for a while. I thought maybe James was asleep, but then I realized he had a boner. We quickly got undressed. We'd already figured out what to do with each other through trial and error. James's idea of the sexiest thing was what he called a "tongue twisty." I don't know where he came up with that name. I hated the name. It sounded like French kissing, even though James and I had never once kissed.

The next morning, James got out of bed before me. I found him eating cereal in the dining room. It always bothered me when he got up before me and ate cereal. I imagined him picking his nose and getting boogers all over our pantry, even though James stopped picking his nose when it was do-or-die in second grade.

"What are we doing today?" James asked with cereal in his mouth.

"*I'm* going to work on my novel," I said, already thinking about Beverly. I needed a plot twist about bad wishes coming true. Then I realized that my wish to have James sleep over was bad and *it* had come true; I had sinned against the Father Almighty!

"I'm bored," James said, the moment he finished his cereal.

"Can't your dad come pick you up?" I asked.

"I don't want to call him."

"Well, I'm sure my dad will take you home when he gets up."

James watched cartoons while I worked on my novel. I wrote a long conversation between Beverly and Craig about what kinds of wishes might be bad, but they decided not to worry about it. Beverly made lunch for the two of them and began teaching herself to sew.

"Look at that!" James said, pointing to a Teenage Mutant Ninja Turtles ad. What a dork!

Working on a novel was way better.

"You ready to go home, James?" my dad asked.

"Yeah, I suppose," James sighed.

"See ya later," I said, wanting him to leave as quickly as possible.

"You're not coming with us?" Dad asked.

"I'm working on my novel."

"All right. Come on, James."

Once they were gone I grabbed the TV remote and sat in my dad's recliner. Mom came into the living room. "Did you have fun with James?" she asked.

"Yeah. It was all right."

"That poor kid," she said, like she was talking to a room full of people. Sometimes Mom was weird, but at least she wasn't as bad as James's mom. James's mom was wacko. I couldn't stand James's family. Again, I thought about the midnight sex games James and I played. It was nothing new.

I imagined playing those games with Mark instead.

* * *

Upstairs in my bedroom I pulled out all of my old artwork and began to reminisce. I decided I wanted to start drawing again. I found some paper and a pencil and thought about what to draw. I doodled a few made-up cartoon characters and imagined their conversation. I really wanted to draw a picture of Mark so that I could look at it instead of just having to imagine him all the time. My only fear was that someone would find it and know I was a big faggot. I decided to draw it anyway.

I found a fresh piece of paper and moved my typewriter off my desk. I closed my eyes and thought about Mark doing it with me. It took me a minute to mentally dress him for the portrait. Once I had it, I began to draw. Every time I made a mistake I crumpled the paper and started over. Finally, I had it in full color and it was dazzling. Mark was on a football field holding the ball in one hand, like a knight lowering his sword after he's won the battle. I'd captured his lips perfectly! I kissed the paper, even though doing it made me feel silly.

"Beverly, this is your prince, go find him."

I folded the picture into tiny squares and hid it under my wooden toy box in the closet.

Chapter 5

When I got to school on Monday, I found Katy and Stacy in the coatroom talking about how Anna and Mark were officially going out. Apparently they'd gone to McDonald's with Doug Swisher and his girlfriend, Amanda Peters, who were in seventh grade. It was there that Mark had supposedly popped the question. I tried to imagine what he might have said. If I were Anna, I would have died right then no matter what he said. But I'm sure she handled it perfectly. Anna was so beautiful. All the girls envied her, especially me. I just knew that she and Mark were going to be so unbearably cute together. Life was so unfair! My parents should never have had me.

On my way to my desk, I saw that James had left his pencil case unattended. I felt like being mean, so I snatched it and hid it in my desk. When he came out of the coatroom, he immediately shouted, "Who stole my pencil case?"

I showed it to Kevin and Brett and they started laughing.

James put his hand on his hip. "Come on, Andy, why do you have to be this way?"

"Who do you think you are—my girlfriend?"

Everyone started laughing at James. I tossed the pencil case to Kevin, who tossed it to Brett, and it was like a hot potato until Sister Mary Kelly came in and caught Mathew with it.

She saw that James was upset and shouted, "Give that back, Mathew!"

Mathew reddened. "Sorry," he said, and the class began to snicker. Mathew was trying not to laugh as he handed the pencil case back to James.

James gave me a final glare and then sat down, acting like *such* a girl. He even had the audacity to cross his legs like a girl. Even Sister Mary Kelly noticed how weird James was acting. James finally sat normally, only to put his face in his hands and start crying. He was making the biggest spectacle of himself!

Sister Mary Kelly began teaching class as usual, and James finally sat up and stared down at his open book, never making eye contact with anyone.

Nancy whispered in my ear. "You're a dick."

When we got into reading groups, Nancy and Anna and all the girls were super nice to James. I sat with the guys. None of them were nice to me. In fact, they acted like I didn't even exist. I so regretted taking James's pencil case. Now everyone knew we were faggots together. I had to end our friendship. We couldn't go on like this and survive.

On my way to detention, Sister Mary Kelly stopped me and said, "Young man, you're going to the principal's office."

Mr. Preston's door had a window in it that you couldn't see through very well—with the kind of frosty glass on a shower door. It said "Principal" in black letters. I knocked on the window and it rattled.

"Come in!" Mr. Preston said.

I entered the room. Mr. Preston was sitting at his desk, facing me with his fingers laced together over an old-fashioned lunch box. He seemed surprisingly pleasant. "Let's have lunch, shall we?"

"I buy my lunch in the cafeteria."

Mr. Preston frowned. "Oh?" An idea came to him. He picked up the phone. "Mrs. Kennedy, would you please send up a hot school lunch?"

Mr. Preston hung up and smiled. "Problem solved."

I slouched in my chair.

"I can tell you don't want to be here," he continued. "I don't blame you. But what would you have me do, considering you were vandalizing the lunchroom?"

"No I wasn't!" I protested.

"Come on now? The pickles?"

I soured. Could that really be considered vandalism? I wondered if the stranger with the broken-down car had ever committed vandalism.

"I know you know right from wrong. So I don't think I need to elaborate any further. You know why you're being punished."

Mr. Preston opened his lunch box and removed its contents. First there was a sandwich, then an apple. Then with a wide grin he pulled out an assortment of little candy bars. Putting a finger to his lips he said, "Don't tell anyone."

"I won't. I promise."

Mr. Preston seemed pleased and opened one of the wrappers. He offered me a piece of chocolate. Then my fish fillet arrived.

"How's the writing coming along?" Mr. Preston asked as we ate our food.

I wasn't too surprised that he asked me about my work. Some of my teachers knew I wanted to be a novelist, because I'd been writing books for the last two years. They had told me that my stories were good but my spelling was horrible, and had asked if I had so much free time to write, then why weren't my assignments ever completed? I felt so rejected. All I ever wanted was for someone to discover me so I would be published. I wondered if that someone would be Mr. Preston.

"It's going good," I told him.

"That's what I hear. Your name sometimes comes up in the teachers' lounge."

"Really?"

"Yes."

I was beaming. This didn't feel like a punishment at all! Mr. Preston was telling me that I was special.

"I've heard that some of the subject matter is violent?"

He was referring to my last novel, when I had gangs of alley cats in a dispute over territory. None of my teachers seemed to understand that the violence was the backstory. The real story was my heroine, Pepper, trying to get her life together after she runs away from the farm with her best friend, Salt.

"I'm pleased to hear that you've developed creative hobbies. I just want to make sure that you take a healthy approach to your writing."

"I write prayers," I said. In third grade, Sister Mary Ruth made everyone write a prayer, and mine got huge attention when Father Frank read it in church. I wrote a few more prayers after that but gave them up to write novels, because prayers are super boring.

"And of course prayer is truly a blessing," Mr. Preston said.

I turned on the charm. "I promise to be on my absolute best behavior for the rest of the year."

"Let's pray you do."

For the rest of the day all I could think about was my conversation with Mr. Preston. I really was sorry and wanted to do better. During science class I put my notebook on my lap and wrote a prayer:

Oh God of wonders! Oh Holy Shepherd, guide me! Bless my ears so that I may hear your word, and bless my mouth so that I may speak it. Bless my pen so that in my writing others will see and hear your glory. And when there is darkness, and temptation lurks within, guide me to do your wishes, wishes that heal, not sin. Destroy sinful wishes and the devil—he knocks at my door. Then I will see your glory forevermore.

I reread my prayer, simply delighted to have used a dash. Those were particularly tricky. The bell rang, and I looked up at the clock. Class had passed me by and I hadn't absorbed any of it. I didn't even know what the homework assignment was. But I was too busy to find out. I just had to work on my novel!

***

When I got home I lay in bed and reread my entire novel with a smile. But when I sat down to write the next scene, I found myself thinking of James. I felt awful for stealing his pencil case. I decided to call him and apologize so he wouldn't hate me.

"Oh, it's you," James said, obviously still upset over it.

"Sorry."

"Why'd you do it?"

"I don't know. . . ."

"I *don't* forgive you."

"What? You *have* to forgive me! Please forgive me. I said I was sorry."

"Why are you so mean?"

"*I* . . . This sucks!" I hung up the phone.

James called back immediately. "I forgive you."

It figured that James would be so immature about everything. "Whatever," I said.

"What are you doing?" he asked.

"Watching TV." Suddenly I was irked. This friendship was stupid. It had to end tonight. "Don't ever call me again!"

"Don't ever call me again either!" James said.

"I hate you!" I said, hanging up the phone before James could respond.

Chapter 6

I was starting to worry about sixth grade. Far from the best year ever, by October I knew it was going to be the worst year of my life. James and I hated each other forever, Mark was busy being a couple with Anna, and no one else would even give me the time of day, because I was the faggot who had pulled Casey Fisher's hair and who had to serve hot school lunch in detention. None of it was my fault! It was so unfair!

When I told Mr. Preston, he said that a lot of writers feel misunderstood. I said that the only reason I threw pickles in the lunchroom was to make people laugh. Mr. Preston called that a "breakthrough" and said that now that I knew the reasons behind my actions, I could learn to make people laugh in ways that didn't vandalize the school. I asked him if he ever had trouble making people like him when he was a kid.

"Oh, I'm sure you'd be surprised, Andy, to know that everyone feels lonely at your age from time to time. And I have to admit I did get a detention or two from acting out. Although, back in my day detention meant having to clap erasers while hanging from the roof by your toes!"

I laughed for about five minutes. Mr. Preston wasn't so bad, I supposed. For sure he wasn't a faggot.

Finally, he told me that I could stop serving hot lunch, my detention was over. If I ever wanted to talk, though, I could stop by his office. He said he enjoyed my conversation, and I wondered if he was lonely. I thought about his secret candy bars. Maybe he was nutty—for a principal.

The following Monday I finally got to join my classmates for lunch and recess. I sat with Mark and all the guys, of course. Meanwhile, James sat all by himself at the end of the fourth-grade table. He didn't dare come over. I wondered why he wouldn't at least sit with the girls or something. Sitting alone was so pathetic. What was James thinking? He was cute! He could be popular—if only he wasn't such a miserable loser from Mars. I felt like telling him to misbehave, because he'd get sent to detention, and he and Mr. Preston were perfect for each other.

"So what's Mr. Preston like in his office?" Kevin asked.

Everyone at the table faced me eagerly.

Not wanting to blow my popularity, I said, "He's pretty faggy. And he eats candy bars for lunch."

"Mr. Preston is a total faggot," Brett said.

We all laughed, except for Mark—Mark said he was sick of that word, and out of nowhere I felt a ton of bricks lift off my back.

I was planning on riding my bike to the triangle after school, but Mark told me no one was going there anymore. I was kind of surprised. I wondered if something had happened between him and Anna.

Mark wouldn't even look me in the eyes. "Naw, it's nothing like that. . . . You can keep sitting with us at lunch, though . . . if you want."

"Um . . . okay," I said, puzzled but glad that I could sit with Mark at lunch.

"Well, anyway, I gotta go. I got stuff to do. . . . You okay?"

"Yeah." Why wouldn't I be? Mark was acting really weird. Again, I wished I were Anna, because then I could just ask him why he was acting so weird and make out with him until he felt better.

"See ya later," Mark said, pedaling away. I watched

him go but stopped when out of the corner of my eye I saw Brett and Mathew exiting the school. If they saw me watching Mark so intently, I'd be killed!

* * *

Beverly sat in her chair trying to sew her red dress but pricked her fingers repeatedly. She was cursed! No matter how hard she tried to be a good girl, bad things were happening to her, such as burning herself on the stove or getting her toe pinched in a mousetrap. It was all because she'd stolen other people's wishes.

"All I ever wanted was to find the boy in the picture," she told Wobblygums. "But by now he's probably got another girlfriend. It's so unfair! I love him!"

"Go back to school, Beverly. If you can't have love, then you have to follow your dreams as a businesswoman," Wobblygums replied.

"I'm going to be the most successful businesswoman ever!" Beverly declared.

They decided to have a tea party, and it turned out to be the height of sophistication.

* * *

Mom would not stop bugging me to let her read my book. But I couldn't show it to her. She would think I'd gone crazy! I wondered if I needed therapy but didn't dare ask. "I'll let you read it when it's finished," I told her. "I want it to be perfect."

"Well, all right," she pouted.

We were both sitting on my bed, next to my type-writer, which was perched on a TV tray because my desk was too messy. Mom wanted me to clean my room, but I was way too busy. I had a novel to write.

"*Roseanne* is on tonight," she said. "You want to come down and watch it with us?"

"Yeah," I said.

"Okay. I love you."

"I love you, too."

I hugged my mom for a long time.

* * *

Now that Mark and Anna were a couple, everyone hung out on the steps at recess instead of playing football. In fact, no one even went to the triangle anymore. I couldn't have been more pleased. I hated sports and found this to be a better way to spend recess. It was a chance to find out how everyone felt about everything.

Katy told a hilarious story about how once when she was on vacation her dad got in a fight with a guy in a gorilla costume in the middle of the street. Kevin did an impression of Katy's dad and everyone laughed their asses off. I was surprised that so many people knew Katy's dad. He sounded scary to me.

Everyone started talking about how Katy's parents were letting her have a boy-girl party. I wasn't officially invited, but it was assumed that I'd be there. No one knew what to wear for Halloween; however, everyone agreed that we were too old for trick-or-treating. It was obvious.

This would be my first boy-girl party, and I began to get nervous about what to wear. I wanted to make a good impression on everyone. Halloween fell on a Wednesday, and that morning I got up an hour early. My plan was to be as gruesome as possible and scare all the girls and teachers. So I used fake skin and makeup to make my face look like it had been sliced up with razors, then added tons of fake blood and safety pins for stitches. My face was *so* scary!

Amy backed away when she saw me in the hallway, but after she realized it was just me, she thought it was really cool. Mom was upset by the costume, saying she wasn't going to let me leave the house. But I insisted that people were supposed to be scary on Halloween, and she finally caved in.

When I got on the bus nearly everyone was in costume, and some of them had intended on being scary, but I was easily the scariest. Even the guys at school were shocked. They couldn't believe I could make it look so real. When Nancy saw me, she got so freaked out that she wouldn't talk to me for the rest of the day. I snuck up on her twice, and she screamed both times.

As the day wore on, the wounds began to droop and

I looked even more hideous. Mrs. Lorenz finally made me wash off my face, because my math paper had fake blood drops on it.

"Why are you such a weirdo?" Nancy asked, now that my face wasn't scary.

"I'm not a weirdo, it's Halloween."

"You're a weirdo year-round."

All the girls, including James, laughed at me. How dare James stab me in the back! When I laughed at him, it was only because he deserved it. I was so glad our friendship was over.

I wondered if James ever missed me.

After school let out I was heading for my bus when Mr. Preston stopped me. "That was a scary costume," he said.

I grinned.

"The *gore,* it looked very real. What made you think of it?"

"Halloween."

"Of course." An awkward moment of silence passed between us. "Behave tonight," he said.

At home I found Dad sitting in his recliner and eating candy from the trick-or-treat bucket. I grabbed a Snickers.

"So," Dad began casually, "your mom tells me you're going to your first boy-girl party tonight?"

I felt trapped. "Yes. . . ."

"Who are you going with?"

The Boys and the Bees

"My friend Mark Saddle."

"Is there a particular girl you're meeting?"

"No . . . I mean maybe." *There's always Casey Fisher.* Suddenly, I could barely keep a straight face. I wanted to laugh out loud but didn't want to hurt his feelings. Poor Dad was just trying to be buds. I almost wished I had a girlfriend so I could tell him all about her and really impress him.

"Have a good time tonight," Dad said. "And stay on your best behavior."

"I will," I said, annoyed that for the second time that day I was being told by adults to behave myself.

* * *

I was drinking a glass of juice in the kitchen when the phone rang. Mom answered it, then handed it to me. "Hello?" I said.

"Hi," James said.

"Oh, hi." I couldn't believe James was actually calling me, even though he almost always was the first to come crawling back after a fight.

"What are you doing?"

"Nothing."

"Are you going to the Halloween party?"

"Yeah, are you?"

"No," he said unhappily. "My parents think we're too young for boy-girl parties."

58.

"Oh well," I sighed. "Maybe next year."

"It's not fair. You get to go."

"Look, James, why are you even calling me? We're not friends anymore."

"Nancy's right. You *are* a weirdo!"

"At least I'm not *you!*" I hung up the phone.

"James isn't going to the party?" Mom asked.

"His parents won't let him."

She sighed. "That poor kid. Why don't you invite him over one of these nights for a sleepover?"

"Never," I said, even though I kind of wanted James to sleep over this weekend. I considered skipping the party and calling James back and finally making up and being friends again—but I couldn't, because I already had my Halloween costume planned. For my daytime costume I had been scary. Tonight I wanted to be sexy. So I was going to dress like the sexiest man of all time: Superman!

I'd purchased the costume from Paper Warehouse with my own money. I was a little bit disappointed with the size of my muscles once I had it on. But the cape was super-cool! Everyone at the party was going to think I was so cute. Maybe even Mark would think that—in my dreams!

Mom drove me to the party. Despite my protests, she made me wear my winter coat. That wasn't such a bad idea after all, because it was so cold outside that I shivered even with the coat on.

When I got to Katy's house a bunch of people were already there, including Mark and the rest of the guys. Katy's mom came to greet me at the door, holding a large glass bowl of baked pumpkin seeds. She told me to put my coat upstairs.

Kevin saw me on my way back downstairs. "*Superman!*" he cried, bursting into laughter.

Everyone at the party faced me, pointed their fingers in my direction and laughed. My face felt like it was melting! I had wanted to be sexy, but I was a freak of nature! Everybody hated me!

I ran upstairs, put my coat back on, and sat on the bed, afraid to be seen as I left. It was so stupid of me to dress like Superman! I should have known. I was such a faggot! I wished I hadn't come to the party. I belonged with losers like James.

Katy's mom came into the room. "I'm so sorry about that. Are you okay?"

I was so embarrassed. "Yes. . . ."

"Katy came up to apologize," she added, pulling Katy into the room.

"*Sorry,*" Katy said begrudgingly, then biting her lip to keep from smiling.

Katy's mom tried to help. "Do you want to come back down and join the party?"

I shrugged.

"Do you want to go home?"

"I don't know."

Katy groaned, sounding more fed up with me than ever. "Can I go back to my party now?"

"*Fine,*" her mom said curtly.

I sat for a minute alone with her mom standing over me, then said, "I'll go back down." I kept my coat on and started down the stairs. Everyone was watching me again, only they weren't laughing this time. Actually they were trying *not* to laugh.

Mark greeted me at the bottom of the stairs, chuckling, "That's a wild costume, man. Glad you got the coat on."

I smiled in spite of myself.

Mark put his arm around my shoulder. It was happening! He was taking me under his wing for real. We joined the rest of the guys, and no one teased me. Maybe Mark or Katy's mom or someone had told them not to. Soon it just felt like we were at school again.

We went outside to Katy's backyard. It was dark out. Mathew grabbed one of the aluminum trash cans in the alley behind Katy's house and threw it up against someone's garage. It crashed so loud that everyone covered their ears. We were all freaking out and laughing as we ran to the end of the block before anyone came out of their house to yell at us.

When we got back to Katy's house her parents were enraged. One of the neighbors had called because they'd heard the trash can and seen us running away—as if half the neighborhood was already in bed at 9:00 P.M. Katy's mom made us call home for rides. Naturally, everyone told their parents that they didn't know who threw the trash can.

Sister Mary Kelly had heard about the trouble and was furious that someone had thrown a trash can. The next day before morning prayer she suggested that perhaps we weren't old enough yet to be having boy-girl parties. This of course made everyone speak of the incident as legendary, and I was so glad that I'd gone to the party. Now I wished that I had been the one to throw the trash can.

At recess James stopped me on my way to the steps. He wanted to talk. "Why are you being so mean to me? I'm your best friend."

"James, I'm not trying to be mean to you," I said. "I'm just trying to live my life, and I can't help it if your parents won't let you go to parties."

"That's not even what I'm talking about."

"Then what *are* you talking about?"

"I'm talking about . . . I thought that . . . you liked me. . . ."

"I don't like you! *Eew.*"

James looked wounded and pathetic. I wished he'd just stand up to me for once. Sometimes I even wished we could just beat each other up.

"We seriously can't be friends anymore," I said. "You're too much of a girl."

James turned angry. "Don't you even realize what a

moron you are, Andy? Don't you realize that those people aren't even your friends? That they all go to the triangle without you because the guys told Mark they wouldn't play football if you played?"

"You're lying!"

"Go see for yourself . . . *asshole!*"

"Fuck you!" I said, storming off to the other end of the playground and hiding behind the building so no one would see me so angry.

The moment I got home after school, I hopped on my bike and headed for the triangle. I took the longest route I could think of, because I didn't want anyone from school to see me biking alone. I parked my bike and hid behind a tree. There they were, the guys and girls of my class. The girls had on cute coats, and the guys played football in sweatshirts and winter hats. I stared at Mark. Mark! Oh, Mark! He was the only boy not wearing a hat, and his sandy blond hair was all ruffled. I just wanted to run my fingers through it. It was my only wish.

I realized suddenly that I had picked a long strip of bark off the tree I was hiding behind. I got on my bike and pedaled home. Lying in my bed with my face in the pillow, I thought about how everyone had lied to me about going to the triangle, and I wept.

I decided I hated my novel.

Chapter 7

On the night of the first snowfall I grabbed a blanket, sat in my dad's recliner, and discovered my new favorite TV show—*Beverly Hills 90210*. There was a character in it, Brandon Walsh, and whoever played him was so unbelievably cute that every time he was on the screen I just wanted to squeeze him. Then someone spiked his drink at a party and he got into a car crash. I was so shocked, it made me cry. I hoped they'd make an episode about cigarettes one day.

The show lasted until 10:00 P.M., but at 9:35 Dad

told me it was past my bedtime, which was 9:30 on a school night, and that I had to turn off the TV and go to bed.

"But I'm eleven years old! Everyone else in my grade stays up as late as they want!"

"In this house, eleven-year-olds go to bed at nine-thirty on school nights."

"You're so unfair!" I cried, sulking up to my room. Now I'd never know how the show ended.

At recess the next day, talking to Mark and all the guys, I realized how obvious it was that they were lying to me about playing football at the triangle. They didn't know that I'd spied on them from behind a tree. Mark acted like there wasn't even a secret to keep. He was as nice as usual, but now I knew how he really felt. I couldn't stand to be around the guys anymore.

For the first time all year I sat with James for lunch. "I knew you'd come back," James said, forgiving me on the spot.

I smiled at him wearily. "James, I know I've been a huge creep this year, but things are going to change. I swear."

"Okay."

Then it dawned on me. "Oh my God, there's this new show on called *Beverly Hills 90210*. You would seriously freak!"

* * *

A couple of weeks later I slid my feet through the snow on the way to the bus. Mark stopped me to ask why I hadn't been sitting with him and the rest of the guys at lunch. I blushed and said, "No reason."

"Oh, well, we miss you. You're the funny guy."

I thought that was a polite way of saying I'm a faggot.

But Mark had smiled at me. He still liked me! I was so overjoyed that I thought I might cry right then and there and ruin everything. I concentrated on the black snow under the wheel of the bus.

"You okay?" Mark asked.

"I heard you guys still go to the triangle."

Mark frowned. "Oh man . . . sorry about that."

"It's no big deal. I know I suck."

"Didn't you say you wanted to play basketball this year?"

"Yeah. . . ."

"You should come over to my house sometime and we can play one-on-one. I'll teach you some moves." He smacked me on the arm jovially and I almost fell over.

"See ya," he said.

When I got home I ran straight to my room and found the picture I had drawn of Mark on the football field. I lay in my bed and looked at it for what must have been a half hour. Then I closed my eyes and thought about Mark teaching me basketball. Maybe I'd be good and sixth grade really would be my best year ever. I pictured the camaraderie of the team. Everyone would want to be my friend at last.

I found some paper and drew another picture of Mark. He was in the locker room in his basketball uniform with war paint under his eyes. He looked so good. I crawled under my covers with the drawing and pretended my hand was Mark's hand.

James felt betrayed when I didn't sit with him at lunch the next day. "You said you wouldn't be mean to me anymore."

"I'm not being mean."

"You're avoiding me again."

"What am I supposed to do, avoid Mark and those guys? That would be rude."

"How can you hang out with them when all they do is make fun of us?"

"Speak for yourself, faggot!"

I got to music class just as Mrs. Ruff began to play a few notes on the piano to get everyone's attention. I waited for James to come in, but he didn't. I felt disgusted with myself for acting the way I did. I really was such a terrible friend!

As the class sang Christmas music, I thought that James was actually fortunate to be absent, because he had the highest singing voice among the guys and always got teased. Would it always be this way? I was terrified about being eleven but even more terrified of growing up.

* * *

Mark approached me the next day outside of science class. "Hey, man, you wanna come over to my house after school and shoot hoops?"

I choked up instantly and stammered, "Yeah, I can come."

Kevin and Brett grunted. They were walking ahead of us, and I was pretty sure they laughed at Mark's offer. The only thing more ridiculous would have been to invite James.

Brett turned to me. "Dude, are you sure you're not completely hopeless on the court?"

I had to stand up for myself. "Are you sure *you* can keep up?" I asked boldly.

Mark warned him off. "He won't be able to if he doesn't practice."

Suddenly Anna was at Mark's side, wrapping her arms around his waist. "Whoa!" Mark cried out, laughing.

"I, like, don't even think I can deal with science," Anna said to no one in particular. "What are we doing after school today?"

"I'm playing hoops with m' bud here," Mark answered, clapping me on the shoulder.

Anna eyed me with a smirk. "Andy, are you really going to play basketball this year?"

I blushed. "Yeah. . . ."

Everything came to a stop, however, when Mr. Preston came around the corner. "Andy, I need to have a word with you in my office."

We spazzed out silently, making lots of wild eye contact that said, "What the hell?"

"What'd Andy do?" Mark asked.

For a moment I thought my heart would pop as I waited for Mr. Preston to respond.

Mr. Preston replied, "This doesn't concern you, Mark."

"See ya, man," Mark said, speeding away along with everyone else as if a bell had rung.

I followed Mr. Preston to his office.

"I suppose you're wondering what now?" he asked.

I shrugged. I couldn't begin to guess.

"I'm disappointed that you can't figure it out for yourself. James came to my office today. He was very upset. He told me you called him a bad word."

So James had ratted me out! My face burned with guilt. I couldn't look Mr. Preston in the eye. Boy, he must have felt let down by me.

"Do you know what that word means?"

He was trying to get me to confess. I said nothing but instead damned James over and over.

"Well, it's not a very nice word for homosexuals, and I refuse to tolerate it being used in this school. It's the same as using a racist slur."

"But—"

"No buts about it."

I was only trying to tell him my side of it. Everyone said the word "faggot." It was the most popular word around school besides "fuck," and I, of all people, should not be held responsible for it. I got called a faggot all the time. Why hadn't anyone come to *my* rescue when *I* got called that?

"Do you promise me that from now on you won't use that word?"

"Yes," I said, so embarrassed I wanted to die. After the nice things Mr. Preston had said about my writing, here I was in trouble with him. I felt like such a faggot. It was all James's fault.

I sat there in silence until Mr. Preston finally asked, "Are you all right?"

"I'm fine," I muttered.

He sighed. "Off to class."

When I got to my classroom, late, I sat at my desk and thought hard about what a disappointment I was to Mr. Preston. Somehow his approval meant more to me than anyone else's, except Mark's. But that reminded me that I was going to Mark's house after school to play basketball. The day wouldn't be a disaster after all.

When school ended for the day, I looked everywhere for Mark. Finally I spotted him saying good-bye to Anna, who was getting on her bus. I waited until she was gone, of course, to approach him. I was really nervous about spending so much time alone with him. What a relief when he smiled at me!

On the way to his house Mark told me that he'd taught his little sister how to play basketball, and he'd be able to teach me. He said I had a good frame for it. What did *that* mean? If anyone but Mark had said it, I'd have called it gay. He told me his sister was six, which was the same age as Amy. I would have mentioned the coincidence, but I was too shy. Besides, getting compared to his six-year-old sister was kind of embarrassing.

When we got to Mark's house we didn't go inside. Instead, we went to his backyard. I was glad about it, too, because I remembered hearing that Mark's dad was super strict. Actually, I didn't want to meet anyone in Mark's family. I feared them, just because they had so much influence on Mark, and other people's parents always seemed to hate their kid's friends. James's family always acted like they wished I'd never been born.

Mark threw his bike onto the lawn. "Come on, let's shoot hoops."

The basketball hoop was attached to the garage. Around the roof and all throughout the bushes were Christmas lights, which Mark switched on. "My dad put these up," he said, impressed by his father's know-how.

We threw our coats over the fence. The court had been shoveled but was still wet from snow. Mark dribbled the ball smoothly, coming at me and spinning around me to sink a basket as if I weren't even standing there. Every time he jumped, his shirt rose up on his body, exposing his waistline. His skin fascinated me, and I wondered what the rest of his body looked like under his clothes.

"Come on, man, what're waiting for?" Mark asked, like I was his six-year-old sister. "Come and get it."

I tried for the ball, but Mark spun again, brushing up against me this time. I was suddenly so turned on that I was sure he would be able to tell just by my face.

"Try again," Mark said, still dribbling.

I moved toward him, reaching for the ball.

"Nice try, sucka," Mark said, sinking another basket.

I started laughing. "Shouldn't I get a handicap?"

"Here, you shoot," he said, tossing me the ball.

At least I caught it. Surprisingly, I was good at dribbling—as long as no one tried to get the ball from me. Although I aimed for the basket, the ball bounced off the top of the backboard.

"Nice try," Mark said, throwing me the ball again.

He showed me where to stand for a lay-up and the exact spot to aim at. I must have done it a hundred times before I actually got the ball in.

"That's where you'll stand when I pass to you during a game," he said, pointing to the spot in the driveway where I stood.

"No way, man. I'll pass it to you."

"I wouldn't want to hog the ball."

"Do you really think I'll ever be good?" I asked.

"Yeah, man, you've got the raw talent."

A good frame, raw talent—Mark was really turning me on.

He caught me staring at him for too long, and we both looked away at the same time, almost pretending that I wasn't looking and that he didn't know I was looking. Sometimes Mark seemed just as embarrassed to be with me as I was to be with him—unless it was all in my head, which it might have been. No way was I going to ask him about it.

We played a game of one-on-one. Mark let me have the ball first, and he got so close before stealing the ball that I could feel his skin next to mine. I'd find reasons to touch him on his back and stuff, sometimes even letting my hand linger. I almost felt guilty about what I was doing, because I was certain he was going to yell at me or something.

As for who won the game, Mark only let me score when he was being nice. But to me, the game had nothing to do with basketball. It was my first chance to be alone with Mark. So if you asked me, *I* was the real winner.

* * *

That night I set my typewriter on a TV tray in my bedroom and checked to see where I had left off on my novel. I'd seriously let my writing slip. "Oh, yeah," I groaned, wondering what on earth I could have Beverly do about being cursed. It was time for her luck to change. She was going to find the boy in the picture.

As Beverly trotted along the trail, Wobblygums flew down and fluttered his wings. "Beverly, don't leave the forest! It's dangerous in town!"

"But I must find the boy I seek."

"Why?"

"Because I love him."

I stopped typing and started at the page. *I love him.* My heart clenched.

Chapter 8

Mark coached me two more times before the season started. James was annoyed to find out that I was trying out for the team, but I wasn't like him, I said. I actually had a chance of being one of the cool kids.

At our first official practice, Coach Pooch lined us up as though he were a drill sergeant. He shouted that our first game was in only two weeks and that we should have been practicing every day for the last two months. He didn't mention that it was not the players who had fumbled the scheduling but took it out on us nonetheless.

Coach Pooch had his assistant, Red, pass out team uniforms, which we had to change into in the locker room before practice. I'd never seen any of the guys naked before, much less all of them at once. I wanted to take a peek but was terrified of getting caught—of proving I was a fag—and mostly looked at my locker, listening to the sound of laughter and clothes hitting the concrete floor.

The second I heard Mark's voice to my left, I glanced very casually to see him pulling his jersey over his head. His chest looked nothing like James's or mine. He looked like an athlete.

Once practice got under way it was apparent immediately that I was the worst player. Coach Pooch yelled at me, which made the guys laugh. It could have been worse, I guess. At least I was *on* the team.

After two hours of running laps and throwing basketballs across the room, I was so exhausted that I almost didn't notice the sound of Coach Pooch's whistle. "All right, that's enough for tonight. I want all of you here same time tomorrow, and be prepared to go for an extra hour. Some of you need *a lot* of practice if you want to be in the game, and I only want you to be here if you're serious about the game. I want *you* to love *me* because you love the game. Go Markers!"

Later outside some of the guys made fun of Coach

Pooch's speech. Brett said that the coach and Red were probably faggots. But after a quick deliberation, it was decided that they weren't faggots, they were just assholes.

Mark complimented me on scoring a few baskets and told me I'd improve if I came over to his house again. Mark believed I could play basketball—that was all the support I needed to go forward.

* * *

Our first game was on a Tuesday night. We were up against Our Lady of Peace, which we'd heard was a tough team. It was in our gymnasium, so all the girls were coming to support us. They all acted like it was the biggest deal ever.

At lunch, Anna told me that if Coach Pooch actually let me play (which she doubted he would), I should pass the ball to Mark because he'd know what to do with it. Anna always made me look like a loser in front of the guys, but I didn't argue. Mark was my best friend and the best player on the team. I didn't need her telling me to pass it to him. That was already my plan.

The game was scheduled to begin at 7:00 P.M., and we gathered in the gymnasium in our uniforms to do warm-ups a half hour early. The visiting team soon arrived and did warm-ups on the other side of the court. They looked intimidating to me, but so was everyone on my own team. All the players intimidated me.

Once spectators started showing up, I spotted my mom and dad and Amy. Mom waved, and I waved back discreetly, hoping she wouldn't embarrass me in front of my team by taking pictures or something stupid. I didn't need Mom's help to humiliate myself.

James came in by himself. I never would have guessed that he'd show up. He shouted something, but I pretended I hadn't even seen him. I figured he'd sit all alone as usual, but instead he sat with Anna and the girls. Maybe my prayer for James had worked. I prayed once more that he wouldn't do anything too stupid without me there to protect him.

Coach Pooch gathered us around him. "Okay, men, this is one of the most important games of the season. It's our chance to show everyone who's boss. After tonight I want all the other teams to squirm when they hear how tough we are. I can't promise that all of you will get to play tonight," he looked right at me, "but I'll do my best to make sure we fight through this game as one team, one body, like Jesus said. Now get out there and kick ass! Gooooo Markers!"

The first string took the court. I hated seeing Brett out there. It was unfair that the shortest guy in our grade was a first-string basketball player. He was fast, though, and willing to play dirty. Brett kind of scared me sometimes, actually.

Mark played center, of course, and looked perfect in his uniform. The kid he was up against acted nervous.

The moment the game started, Mark got the ball and passed it to Kevin, who made a basket before the other team knew what had hit them.

"Take that!" Coach Pooch shouted from the side-lines. Everyone on the bench, including me, stood up to cheer. The five guys out there gave each other high fives. Then Mark gave Kevin a quick hug. I'd never seen Mark hug anyone before! Not even Anna. I had to get in that game!

The players got back into position. The whistle blew and Mark again got the ball. He passed it to Brett, who passed it to Mathew. Our opponents doubled up on covering Mathew, trying to steal the ball. But he passed it to Mark, and Mark scored from the three-point line.

Everyone stood up and cheered. The game had only just started, and already I was sure we were going to win! I realized that I kind of liked basketball.

The score in the last quarter was 71 to 22. We were killing them. Coach Pooch must have realized that with a lead like that we'd certainly win, so with less than a minute to go he put me in the game. I was scared dumb but went out onto the court. I was playing offense in case Mark could get me the ball and give me the chance to score. We had practiced this so many times at his house that I thought I might be able to pull it off for real. But deep down I knew I was going to make a fool of myself. My only hope was that anything I screwed up wouldn't hurt the score. I sensed my family and James watching me intently, and I imagined them waiting breathlessly for me to embarrass myself. Probably the whole school was.

Mark stood in the center, nodding to each one of his teammates. When he saw me, he smiled. I blushed and then turned to face my opponent, who was twice my size with a dark brown flattop haircut and a fierce grimace. He probably wanted to kill me out of revenge. But before I could run and hide, the whistle blew and the guy checked me, nearly knocking me onto the floor.

"Foul!" the ref yelled, stopping the game with his whistle.

"*Faggot,*" the guy mouthed at me, swaggering over to his teammates, who for the first time all night gave each other high fives.

My first thought was how had he known? Was it written on my face? The audience was booing, and at first I thought they were booing at me. Then I realized they were booing at the kid who'd checked me. I was being awarded a penalty shot.

Getting a free-throw shot was maybe even worse than screwing up in the middle of a play. Suddenly the whole gym was watching me. If I missed, *everyone* would see what a loser I was. The audience quieted down so I could concentrate. I could feel Mark staring at me, and it felt almost as if we were alone. Like no one else in the building mattered—or even existed—for that timeless few seconds.

I must have been taking too long, because Anna cheered, "You can do it, Andy!"

"Go Andy," Katy and Stacy joined in.

Suddenly everyone in that gymnasium started chanting my name: "An-dee! An-dee! An-dee!" Now Mark and I weren't alone. I had the entire audience in my head.

I stared at the rim of the basketball, with the ball positioned at my chest. Mark had made me shoot baskets from this angle a hundred times, and I knew exactly where to aim and how hard to throw the ball. If I could just hit the rim—that might be good enough.

I lifted my arms and threw the ball . . . *swoosh!* It went in! And then the buzzer rang. Game over.

The crowd went wild. My teammates ran up to me and huddled around, cheering. Best of all, Mark had his arms around me. I was pressed against his body, forced there by the fact that Brett and Kevin and everyone else had piled on.

"I knew you could do it!" Mark said, hugging me tighter still. I never knew how good scoring could make a guy feel.

Chapter 9

Christmas was almost here. All the lawns, trees, and roofs were blanketed in snow, and the streets were slick with ice. In front of our church was a life-size nativity scene, which was the school's pride and joy. In fact they guarded the thing so carefully that you'd have thought it was the real baby Jesus inside. Every day someone made sure the statues were clean, and at night they had motion detectors everywhere so that an alarm would go off if hoodlums, chiefly eighth graders, tried to mess with the statues. Some kids once threw snowballs at the nativity scene—risky business, since that alone was cause for suspension.

Sister Mary Kelly decided that this year it would be fun to do Secret Santas, which meant we all had to write our name down on a piece of paper and throw it in a hat. Then we would each draw a name from the hat and give a present to that person on the day before Christmas break.

When the hat came to me, I dipped my fingers in, praying I'd pick Mark's name. When I unfolded the paper, my heart sank. I had drawn James's name!

I looked across the room at James, who was sitting at his desk, eyeing the name he'd drawn with a grin. I was suspicious immediately. He better not have drawn my name. The last thing I needed was some crappy gift from James, like the Teenage Mutant Ninja Turtles drawing he gave me for my last birthday. He noticed me staring at him and blushed. Meanwhile, Mark and Kevin were snickering over the names they had drawn.

"No telling anyone who you picked!" Sister Mary Kelly ordered. "I want the Secret Santas to be top secret until the last day of the semester, when we'll exchange gifts."

On our way to lunch, Mark asked me, "Who'd you draw?"

I sighed. "*James.*"

Mark pretended not to notice my despair. "I got Katy," he grinned.

"I got Stacy," Brett said.

Kevin moaned. "What the hell am I gonna get Nancy?"

"Man, I can't believe we all drew girls' names," Brett said.

"Andy drew James's name," Mark volunteered.

"My point exactly."

The guys laughed. As if on cue, James came around the corner and stopped. Everyone gaped at him, just waiting for him to do something for us to laugh at. Instead James walked past us and headed for the boys' bathroom.

"Hey, faggot, no girls allowed!" Brett shouted.

James pretended not to hear and let the bathroom door shut behind him without looking our way.

"Knock it off, Brett," Mark scolded. "He isn't a faggot."

"That's what you said about Andy."

The guys howled in laughter.

Urgh! How many times would I have to defend myself against that word? Apparently, being on the basketball team and scoring the winning point wasn't enough to protect me. "Go to hell, Brett," I said, "your mom looks lonely down there."

"Ooh, good one!" Brett said sarcastically.

"Enough, you guys," Mark said. "We've got the team to think about."

After school I caught up with Mark on the way to

practice. He was alone, and he asked if I'd seen Brett and the other guys anywhere. I hadn't.

On our way out of the building we heard a muffled scream coming from a stairwell below. Mark peered over the edge of the railing, and what he saw made him shout, "Leave him alone!"

Mark dashed down the stairs. I followed. We found James on the floor in the fetal position with Kevin, Brett, and Mathew standing over him. James was disheveled, and it was clear that there'd been a fight.

"He was staring at my dick in the bathroom, man," Brett shouted.

"Get the fuck out of here!" Mark said.

"Fuck this," Brett replied, and the guys took off.

I should have been mad at the guys, but instead my anger was directed at James. I wanted to shout, "What the fuck is the matter with you?" because his indiscretion would only keep the faggot comments coming at me, too.

"I didn't do it . . . I swear . . . I didn't," James sputtered.

Mark and I helped clean him up and then told him to go home. Although Mark tried to reassure James that everything would be okay, he still cried his eyes out. And to be honest, seeing him cry made me want to cry, too.

Mark was really upset and asked me if I thought he should tell Coach Pooch about the incident. He felt that Brett and the other guys should be punished for beating up defenseless James.

I agreed that it had been cruel of them to attack

James but warned Mark that it might make things worse—for the team—if he told on them, because it had nothing to do with basketball.

Mark didn't like it, but he agreed.

James didn't tell on Brett either. Instead, when anyone asked him about his black eye, he claimed to have fallen down the stairs. No one bothered to question his lie, even though it was obvious that he'd been beaten up. The only thing that changed for James was that Mark insisted on everyone being nicer to him. In fact, he invited him to sit with the rest of us at lunch. I think I was the only one besides Mark who paid James any attention at that table. He hardly made a peep.

Eventually, Kevin decided to poke fun and said, "Hey James, say 'She sells seashells by the seashore.'"

James snapped back, "I'm not going to say that, Kevin."

"Leave him alone," Anna said, which was actually pretty nice of her. Not that the most popular girl had to worry about some dumb boy crossing her.

James must have been embarrassed by the attention, because he spilled his milk.

"Hey, ya creep!" Katy screamed, as she leapt to her feet to wipe milk off her skirt.

"Sorry, Katy," James mumbled.

By now at least half the table was laughing. Mark implored everyone to stop, while I shrank in my seat to avoid the line of fire once again.

"You guys are despicable!" James lisped, running away.

Everyone laughed about James's outburst for the rest of the day—except for Mark.

* * *

When the day arrived to exchange Secret Santas, I realized I had forgotten to get James a gift! All around me everyone ran to one another's desks dropping off little gifts. Molly Purdy put one on my desk. It was a small box wrapped in reindeer-covered wrapping paper. I glanced at James. He'd probably already dropped off his gift, because he was sitting at his desk waiting patiently.

James's smile slackened as everyone took their seats to open gifts and he realized there was nothing for him. Melody Fortune raised her hand, pointing to James. "Sister Mary Kelly, James didn't get a gift."

"All right," she asked like a referee, "who didn't get James a gift?"

"I forgot," I said meekly, which made the class giggle.

"Well, then, you'll have to share your gift with James," Sister Mary Kelly said.

I brought James my gift and set it on his desk, then returned to my seat wishing I'd never *heard* of Secret Santas. Everyone watched as James unwrapped the gift and pulled out a fancy pen that looked like it was made of green marble.

"I knew you were a writer," Molly whispered to me.

"Thanks," I shrugged, wondering how I would share my pen with James.

"Check this out, everyone," Mark said, standing up and unraveling a scroll.

To my surprise Mark held up one of James's Teenage Mutant Ninja Turtles drawings. I'd seen his drawing hundreds of times before, but this one was different. By the looks of it, James had gone all out for Mark. He'd used markers to make the turtles gleam bright green in the drippy sewer surroundings. It was dazzling.

The entire class moved closer to marvel at James's exquisite talent as though it were a masterpiece. Kids asked Mark who had given it to him.

"It's from James," Mark replied.

"You drew this?" Anna asked James, pointing at the picture.

"Yes," James replied, sounding almost unsure that this was the right answer.

"It's awesome!" Kevin announced.

Mark said he wanted to donate the artwork to the class, so Sister Mary Kelly taped it to the center of the bulletin board, then replaced the school notices all around it.

"Can you make more of these?" Mathew asked James.

"Yeah."

"Hey, man, I wish I'd have known you could do that," Brett said, seeming to forget that he'd just beaten James up.

But neither James nor Mark nor I were going to bring it up. Maybe at last those bullies would leave James alone. Finally people would stop calling him a "faggot," and maybe I, too, would escape that name forever.

Chapter 10

On Christmas morning there was one gigantic present for me sitting under the tree among the bunch of smaller presents for Amy. I squealed with delight before I'd even finished unwrapping my gift. My very own TV! It was nineteen inches, color, and had the coolest remote control. My parents were quick to say that I was almost twelve years old and this gift was their way of telling me I was growing up. Then, as if to counteract their gesture, they said I wasn't allowed to neglect my homework or stay up past my bedtime watching it. Guess I'd have to watch *90210* on the sly.

* * *

Christmas break never lasts long enough. Two weeks later when I returned to school, I was taken aback once again by James's picture of the Teenage Mutant Ninja Turtles hanging in the classroom. If we had forgotten how good the drawing was, we were immediately reminded when we got back to class. Mark told James in front of everyone that seeing how cool it was all over again made him wish he'd taken it home and hung it on his bedroom wall instead. The thought of anything having to do with James in Mark's bedroom was unbearable! I thought I was going to throw up in my own lap. The picture was not *that* good.

To make matters worse, Sister Mary Kelly told us that report cards had gone out in the mail the previous Friday. I sucked in my breath, preparing for bad news. I was sure to lose my new TV as soon as my parents found out about my low grades.

"Included with your report cards is a permission slip for a retreat. Tomorrow we'll all be going across the street to the convent for a class on human sexuality—the birds and the bees," she added with her usual giggle.

The whole class giggled right along with her. I'm sure I wasn't the only one who never expected to hear a nun say those words. But who would have thought the school would let us talk about that stuff in a convent! Naturally, I was nervous. Did they actually expect me to sit with the guys and talk about this stuff? What was there to talk about? Was a teacher going to tell us how to do it? And here I thought nothing would make me look like a bigger loser than basketball.

For the rest of the day the sex-ed retreat became my chief concern and torment, until I got home and found my dad holding my report card. Mom's arms were folded across her chest, and they both wore dark expressions. Apparently I hadn't gotten any *VG*s, which meant "very good," and on the back of the card, where all the performance and behavior grades went, I'd gotten straight Ns, for "needs improvement."

Dad listed them, shouting: "Pays attention in class? *N!* Talks during class? *N!* Completes assignments on time? *N—N! N! N! N! N!*" he roared.

Suffice to say, I went to bed with the words "Things are going to change this semester, or else you'll lose your new TV for good" looming over my head.

The next morning Mom handed me the signed sex-ed retreat form without a word. I didn't say anything about it either and stuffed it in my bag. Quite a few kids were absent from school that day, including James. Some parents obviously didn't want their kids taking sex-ed. I didn't blame them! I began to wonder if my mom had even read what she signed.

At the convent the boys and girls were separated into two classrooms. To make an already awkward situation worse, the school assigned Mr. Preston to teach us. I guess having a priest talk to us about sex would have been even worse.

"Quiet down, boys, and form a circle," Mr. Preston said.

With snickers, jabs to the ribs, and whispered comments, we sat in a circle, and Mr. Preston joined us, sitting pretzel-style. The "birds and the bees" talk turned out to be a discussion of our bodies and having babies. Mr. Preston talked to us like a nice dad, going out of his way to be patient and to make an obviously uncomfortable job bearable. I was embarrassed the whole time, however, wanting Mr. Preston to speak faster just to get it over with. Somehow having Mark there made it even worse, because I thought if I threw him the wrong look at the wrong moment—when Mr. Preston said "erect penis," for example—it would blow my cover.

Then something weird happened. Mr. Preston asked each of us to write down a question about sex. He said not to be embarrassed. He'd not tell anyone's name. I wrote down the first thing that popped into my mind: "Is masturbation a sin?" and threw it into the bucket.

No matter what Mr. Preston told us, I panicked that everyone would figure out that I had written the question and I'd never be able to live it down. Meanwhile,

Brett, Mathew, and Kevin were off to the side cracking jokes about what a big faggot Mr. Preston was.

My face was burning red.

The first question read was mine: "Is masturbation a sin?" The guys giggled and looked around the circle to try to figure out who had asked it. I smirked to hide suspicion. Waving his hand to quiet us, Mr. Preston said, "No, it is not a sin. It's normal for young men who aren't yet married."

I would have breathed a sigh of relief had the next question not been "Is it a sin to be gay?" All eyes immediately turned on me. I felt my chest clenching up. "It wasn't me!" I cried desperately.

"Calm down, gentlemen," Mr. Preston said. "This exercise is not a finger-pointing game. These are serious questions. Any one of you could have asked this."

Somehow that realization had a quieting effect on everyone.

"Now I want all of you to listen to me very carefully. It's not a sin to be gay. People are most likely born that way. They shouldn't be punished for it, even if we happen to disagree with their lifestyle. However, it is a sin to have sex with another man, because sex is a holy union permitted only within the confines of marriage between a man and a woman."

As Mr. Preston talked about how big a sin gay sex was—like I didn't already know it—I could do nothing but stare at my lap, awed. All that mattered to me was that it wasn't James or me who wrote that question. Which meant another boy in our grade was gay.

Chapter 11

No one mentioned the sex-ed retreat after that—at least not in front of me. James tried to pry information out of me about what he missed, but my lips were sealed. I feared that if I told James what Mr. Preston had said about sex being a sin, it would stop him from doing it with me. Plus I didn't want him to know there was another gay boy.

My obsession with who wrote the question was put on hold when Mark pulled a CD out of his Trapper Keeper at lunch. "Hey, you guys, check out what I got at Target last night." I glanced at the cover, surprised to see a baby with a boner swimming toward a dollar bill on a hook.

"Awesome!" Brett shouted.

"I love Nirvana!" Mathew said.

I only nodded my head, since I had never heard of Nirvana and couldn't pretend. How stupid of me to have thought I could be popular without knowing who all the bands were. I wasn't alone, however.

"Who's Nirvana?" James asked.

"*Duh!*" Kevin said. "It's the cool band everyone listens to."

"You'll like them," Mark said to James. "They're sweet."

After basketball practice I went home and counted my money; all but two dollars of it was in change. I grabbed the cordless phone and called my mom at work: "Mom, there's this CD I want to buy with my own money. Can you take me to Target after work?"

"You called me at work to ask me this? The answer is no!"

I tried James. "Hey, do you want to come to Target with me?"

"Target's too far away. My mom won't let me," James said.

"Just tell them that you're coming to my house. Then we'll take the bus there. I'll even pay."

"What do you want at Target?"

"The Nirvana CD."

"Why? Because Mark has it?"

"No, because it's a really good band."

"Have you ever even *heard* their music?"

"Look, if you don't want to come I'll just go by myself."

"No wait—I'll come."

James and I knew we'd get in trouble if our parents found out what we were up to. I was only allowed to take the bus home from my mom's work, and as far as James's parents knew, he'd never ridden a city bus. Plus they had forbidden him from listening to rock music. No wonder James was so clueless.

James and I met at the bus stop, and I gave him a quarter to pay the fare, which was all they charged for kids. I took the window seat, mainly because I knew James would want it. But there wasn't much to see in the slushy streets as we rolled through the ghetto.

The ride took longer than we expected, and the streetlights started to come on. In a weird way, being out after dark like that made the trip even more exciting. It seemed like every clerk and security guard was out to apprehend us on every brightly lit aisle. James collided with a woman's cart.

"Watch where you're going!" she barked.

We ran to the kitchen utensil aisle, laughing a little bit as we caught our breath.

"You're the biggest klutz!" I laughed.

"She came out of nowhere!" James insisted.

"Come on." I took James to the CDs and we picked out a copy of Nirvana's *Nevermind*. The clerk who rang up our purchase sneered at us like she knew we were the two biggest losers in our school. Like working at Target didn't suck. I dumped all my change onto her counter just to annoy her. She counted the coins with a miserable frown.

On the way home I realized that if my mom heard me listening to the CD, she'd know that I'd taken the bus without permission. I asked James if we could listen to it at his house. James said no right away, because in his house rock-and-roll was like the biggest sin ever. Finally I convinced him that his house was perfect because his bedroom was in the attic, and if his mom asked what we were listening to we could just say Español lessons.

"I can't believe you're making me do this," James said, creeping in the front door. "We're going to get caught."

I could hear someone banging in the kitchen while James's baby brother cried his head off.

"*Herb?*" James's mom called to us. Herb was James's dad.

"No, it's James!" James shouted.

"And his ugly, stupid friend!" James's younger brother Frank added, walking into the room.

James's mom appeared with the baby in the crook of her arm. "Oh, hi," she said, eyeing me apprehensively, as if even she was trying to figure out how a sissy like James could have friends. She snapped: "Darn it, Bobby, how many times do I have to tell you to turn off that TV and do your homework! You too, Frank!" For a church lady, she had a real temper.

James's brothers were used to her screaming like that and moped out of the room. James's little sister, Nellie, pulled at her mom's dress. "Not now," James's mom huffed. "Go finish your macaroni art!"

James's mother turned her anger on us next. "Where have you two been?" she demanded.

"At the park," James replied.

"The potatoes!" she shrieked, handing the baby to James and running to the kitchen.

"What's its name again?"

"Daniel."

I smiled at Daniel, then found a stuffed horse to give him. James sat the baby down in his playpen and went for the boom box.

"Come on," he said, and we ran quietly upstairs to the attic.

We couldn't have the volume very high, and the guitar in it was so loud that at first I couldn't even understand what the singer was saying. Then we read the lyrics. They were really cool. We decided we liked the CD a lot. By the third time through, we were convinced that Nirvana was the most awesome band ever. And even if it had turned out that they weren't awesome, they would have still been cool, because Mark liked them.

We were lying on James's bed, side by side on our backs. I could see his Lego ship, his folded laundry, and some drawings he'd made of fighter planes. "Do you have any new Teenage Mutant Ninja Turtles pictures?" I asked.

James rolled over me to get off of the bed. He pulled a pile of papers out of his desk.

"These are really good. You should be a cartoonist when you grow up."

"I'm not very good at doing their hands and feet."

"Yeah, I see what you mean. But you'll get better. It would be so cool if I was a novelist and you were a cartoonist. You could illustrate my books!"

"Okay."

Then I remembered that I didn't want James or anyone else reading my book. "Hey, I have an even better idea! Let's make a comic book! We'll set it on an alien planet and have a war!"

"Yeah!" James said.

"*James!* Mom said I have to take your friend home!" his older brother Peter shouted up the stairs.

"I hate her," James said.

"You don't mean that," I insisted, thinking how much I hated her, too. "What should I tell my mom if she sees the CD?"

"Tell her *I* got it for you," James smiled.

"Ooh, good idea!"

* * *

"*James* bought this for you?" Mom asked, waiting for me to elaborate on my lie. Like some kind of psychic, she had opened my school bag and pulled out the CD. I was sure she didn't believe me. "What a coincidence, since you called me at work today and asked me to buy you a CD."

"I had my own money!"

"That's not the point. The point is that Target is in a dangerous part of town. How did you get there? You better not have ridden your bike through that neighborhood."

"We took the bus."

"Honey!" Mom shouted out to Dad. "Guess who took a bus to Target today without permission?"

Dad appeared at my bedroom door on cue. I wondered sometimes if my parents rehearsed this stuff.

"He also bought *this,*" she said, handing him the CD.

Dad flipped it over a couple times. "We warned you about taking away your TV. So you choose: we take the TV or the new CD."

"I'll keep the CD."

With that, Dad went over and unplugged my brand new TV and carried it away under his arm.

Alone at last, I listened to Nirvana turned way down with my ear next to the speaker. I imagined Mark was at his house doing the exact same thing.

I wanted to tell Mark I'd bought the CD, but I worried that he would think I was listening to Nirvana only because I was obsessed with him. I decided to mention it later, if it ever came up. And it did, only not how I'd have guessed.

"We bought the Nirvana CD last night," James announced at lunch the next day, "and it's really good."

"I told you you'd like it," Mark said.

"It's awesome," James said.

Stupid James! *I* was supposed to be the one to tell Mark!

"*You* like Nirvana, James?" Nancy asked.

"Yeah, really," Brett added.

James didn't respond.

No one did.

In spite of James's lameness, I *was* serious about making a comic book with him. At first I couldn't think of any ideas for a story. But in science class I drew a sorceress and started imagining how evil she was. Then I drew a hero, loosely based on my secret drawings of Mark. I decided to put him in a loincloth.

"Holy shit!" Nancy gasped over my shoulder.

I covered the picture with my arms.

"Look at what he drew," she called to Brett, who pulled the drawings out from under me.

"What the fuck?"

"It's for a comic book!" I explained, grabbing the pictures from him and hastily jamming them in my science book. How could I have been so reckless? Hopefully no one would think anything of it.

By the time we had basketball practice that afternoon, Brett had spread the word about my drawings. Although he hadn't recognized Mark in the loincloth, the fact that I drew a guy in a loincloth at all was enough to convince everyone that I was the one who had asked if it was a sin to be gay at our sex-ed retreat.

"Who's going to read a comic book about a guy in a loincloth?" Brett laughed.

Mathew and Kevin snickered along with him.

"What about Tarzan?" I asked, but that just encouraged them further.

"Shut the fuck up about it," Mark said, "who cares what anyone drew?"

There it was again. Mark coming to my rescue. Now if only he could help me find the other gay boy in our class. Unfortunately, that was something I had to do all on my own.

Chapter 12

I t's my birthday! Today I woke up twelve years old! Last night my dad bought boxes of cupcakes for me to bring to school and pass out to my classmates. Sister Mary Kelly led the class in singing "Happy Birthday," which was really embarrassing because you could tell by how fast everyone sang that all they really wanted was the cupcakes.

Not only was it my big day, but tonight we had a really important home game against St. Anthony's. For some reason Mark assumed that I'd want to play because it was my birthday, and he was going to make Coach Pooch put me in the game. I couldn't very well tell Mark that I'd rather not play. Mark loved the game, and I wanted to feel the same.

At lunch Mark said, "When Coach Pooch puts you in, I'm going to get the ball and pass it to you for a lay-up. It's your strongest shot, and I really want to see you score tonight."

"What if he doesn't make it?" Katy asked.

"Then we might lose the game," Mathew said.

"Hey, don't freak him out!" Mark said. "That's not true, Andy. Coach Pooch won't even put you in the game unless we're winning." He said it thinking it would make me feel good, and not realizing he was only confirming my hopelessness.

No matter what they said, my talent as a basketball player was lousy, yet I was relieved to know that the game wouldn't rest on my shoulders. I kept saying to myself, *It's my birthday. Nothing can go wrong.*

"Just make sure you aim for the right basket," Brett said.

"You can do it," James whispered into my ear, trying to be my friend. My only real friend besides Mark.

"See? Your *boyfriend* believes in you," Kevin said.

Everyone laughed.

"He's not even my friend!" I said, feeling guilty instantly and making plans to apologize to James as soon as everyone left.

James looked like he was going to implode.

"Why are you such a creep, Andy?" Anna asked.

"He knows I'm just kidding!"

James rolled his eyes.

"You two are such a couple of faggots," Brett said for the millionth time.

Mark jumped up. "I'm the captain of this team, and I'm sick of that word! Shut the fuck up about faggots."

No one dared say the word "faggot" for the rest of lunch.

We had some time before the game, and Mark said he wanted to practice my lay-up shot. He pretended he was making a run for it, while I waited for him to pass the ball to me under the basket. Soon, I was making the shot every time. However, it would be different during a game.

After a while Mark said he needed a break. I was sort of suspicious, because Mark didn't *need* breaks. "What do you think I should do about Anna?" he asked.

"What about Anna?"

"I dunno . . . she just gets on my nerves sometimes. It just doesn't feel right, ya know?"

I agreed that Anna would be unbearable to date—but any girl would be unbearable to date. I didn't say that but asked cautiously, "Do you like her? Like, *like*-like her?"

Mark looked down and around. "I don't know. It's not like . . . you know. . . ."

"Like what?"

". . . magic."

I stood frozen for about ten seconds, lost in thoughts about Mark and magic.

As everyone showed up for the game, I frantically tried to figure out magic. Although I'd never had a girlfriend, I knew what it was like to want someone so bad that I couldn't even deal with it. Was that what Mark meant? Would Mark ever understand if I told him that's how I felt about him? Would I ever find someone special—besides James? I was twelve years old today and wanted magic.

Unfortunately, it turned out to be the worst birthday ever! There'd never been a bigger buffoon than me in the history of basketball. Not only did I travel, trip on my own two feet, pass to the wrong team, and miss seven shots (Coach Pooch counted), but I also got in Mark's way and we collided. Neither of us was hurt, but all the girls were like "Poor Mark," and everyone stared at me like I was the anti-Christ.

In spite of my self-sabotage, the game ended with Mark scoring about fifty baskets and our team winning the game by a landslide. Everyone cheered Mark, leaving me out of the circle as they carried him off on their shoulders.

I found my family and pleaded with my parents to take me home.

"My life is over!" I cried from the backseat of the car.

"Now, now," Mom said.

"It's your birthday," Dad reminded me, as if I needed reminding.

"You don't understand! I have to transfer to another school!"

"Don't be ridiculous!" Mom said. "It will blow over."

"Why do you play basketball if you suck?" Amy asked.

"*Amy!*" Mom and Dad shouted in unison.

I stuck my tongue out at Amy. "It's *my* birthday!" I said.

When we got home Mom made dinner, and my grandma and grandpa and aunts and uncles and cousins showed up for a party. They all wanted to hear about the basketball game, until Mom made a face that said "don't ask." The family treated me like a "big boy," until I was so ashamed of myself that I hid in my room until it was time for me to blow out the candles on my birthday cake.

When they sang "Happy Birthday" I felt like the biggest faggot ever, and in order to keep myself from bursting into tears, I bit my upper lip. No one could have guessed how horrible I felt. I thought about how mean I had always been to James and wished I were a nicer person as I blew out all my candles.

* * *

Beverly found a calendar and flipped through it, finding out it was her birthday! She jumped up and down for joy. She was finally twelve years old! She opened the door to her one-room cabin in the woods and called Craig and Wobblygums and all her other critter friends into the cabin. Everyone was too busy to join her though.

Sitting in her rocking chair with her sewing, she looked around the cabin. Even with all she had made for her home, she felt it remained desolate. She sighed and thought about the boy in the picture. She was sure his name was Mark. She was sure he would come live in her cabin and it would be the best year ever.

Then again, maybe she *wasn't* so sure. That's when she realized that everybody hated her!

* * *

I stopped writing with tears steaming down my cheeks. It couldn't be! I wouldn't let it end this way.

* * *

There was a knock on her door. Beverly set her things aside and went to answer it.

"Surprise!" Wobblygums and everyone else shouted. Craig was holding a triple-tiered strawberry birthday cake with twelve sparkling candles. "Happy birthday!" they sang.

Beverly cried tears of joy. For the first time in her life she had true friends and all she felt was happiness.

Chapter 13

I felt terrible about how everything had turned out on my birthday. I decided to apologize to James for being mean all the time, and to Mark for crashing into him during the game. I talked to Mark first.

"Sorry about last night."

Mark grinned. "Don't sweat it, man. We all have our bad days."

"Don't you think I should quit the team?"

"Hell no!" Mark insisted. "You can't quit 'cause of just one game."

For some reason it was important to Mark that I stay on the team. I wanted to kiss him. "But Mark, there's no way Coach Pooch will ever put me in a game again. I'm the biggest loser ever."

"It's *our* team! And even if you don't always see game time, we need you there for moral support."

"Whose? Everyone hates me."

"I don't."

Well, that was a relief. But if he didn't hate me, did he like me enough to one day love me? "I guess I won't quit the team," I said.

"Awesome. Let's go get some lunch."

Anna approached us in the lunch line. "Mark, you didn't wait for me," she whined.

"I didn't see you," Mark explained.

"You didn't *see* me?"

"You're not the only thing in my life."

"What are you saying?"

"That there are more important things in life."

Anna huffed in disbelief. Then looking over at me, she said, "Maybe you just like hanging out with faggots."

Before Mark could reply, Anna stormed off.

"It's your own fault, Mark," Nancy explained. "Anna's high maintenance."

"What's that supposed to mean?"

"*Yeah,*" Nancy replied.

Brett stepped in. "I think you're awesome, Nancy."

She grabbed Brett by his shirt collar and pulled him

into a sloppy, lip-smacking kiss. I wanted to throw up right there. Nancy was the meanest girl and Brett was the meanest guy. If those two were going to be a couple, I knew my life could potentially go to hell.

"I don't need a girlfriend," Mark said to no one in particular.

Brett looked my way. "You better not be getting turned on, faggot."

"I fucking *told* you not to use that word!" Mark shouted.

"Why don't you go tell Coach Pooch?" Brett shot back.

"Maybe I will."

Anna, Katy, and Alexandria passed us with their arms linked. Anna yelled out for everyone to hear, "Mark Saddle is a faggot!" The girls broke into giggles and scattered.

"Is that why you hate the word?" Brett boldly asked Mark. "You're a faggot, too?"

Mark tackled Brett, whose tray sailed over his head, splattering everyone in line behind him with spaghetti.

Brett punched Mark, and the lunchroom burst into a chorus of "Fight! Fight! Fight!"

Mrs. Pringles ran over, blowing her whistle. The two boys separated. "Did you start this?" she asked, her eyes blazing at Mark.

Mark nodded.

"Mark Saddle! I'm ashamed of you! I can't believe you of all people would do something like this!"

"He had it coming," Mark said.

Mrs. Pringles ordered Brett and Mark out of the cafeteria. "We'll see what Mr. Preston thinks you two have coming!"

I worried all day about what Mr. Preston would do to Mark. Hopefully, he'd understand that Brett deserved exactly what Mark had dished out. One of Mr. Preston's missions was to get people to stop calling one another "faggot." But if he didn't approve of pickles being thrown in the cafeteria, he certainly wasn't going to approve of fighting.

I finally saw Mark on his way to basketball practice. His face looked hard as stone. Clearly the situation was bad, maybe even worse than I had guessed.

"What happened?" I asked.

"He called my dad," Mark answered mechanically.

"Oh no!"

"*Fuck!*" Mark forced the word through his teeth. "My dad already *thinks* I'm a fucking faggot."

How could anyone ever think Mark was a faggot, least of all his own dad?

"I'm gonna get killed when I get home," Mark said.

Just then Anna walked past. "We're over!"

"*Fine,*" Mark snapped.

"You're a creep!" she shouted as she headed down the hall.

"How come girls have to be so annoying?" Mark asked.

"I don't even like girls," I said.

"I don't either," Mark admitted.

* * *

We should have known that basketball practice would be pretty awful. Brett had a black eye, and surprisingly all the guys took his side. I'm sure Anna had helped trash Mark. And which one of the guys was going to turn against the most popular girl in our grade?

With his back to us, Brett said loud enough for only us to hear, "Mark Saddle is a faggot!"

My response was immediate and enraged. "No, he's not! Take it back!"

"Or what?"

"Or you'll leave here with two black eyes, you fuckin' raccoon!"

Some of the guys laughed, though I wasn't sure if it was at Brett or me.

"Take it back!" I shouted, as much for Mark as for all the times I had been called a faggot. I was suddenly wild with rage. I didn't wait for Brett to take it back. I lunged at him with all my might, and we tumbled down to the floor together, rolling around. When Brett punched me in the face, I punched him back so hard I thought I broke my hand.

Before Mark could jump in, Coach Pooch tore us apart from each other. I didn't wait to hear what he had to say to me. Maybe I'd get thrown off the team or even suspended from school. I didn't care at that moment. Instead, I dashed out of the gym before Coach Pooch could say a word.

At home I locked myself in the bathroom. Brett had bloodied my nose, but the bleeding had stopped on my walk home, and once I washed my face I was relieved that no one would be able to tell.

James called that night. "I want to call Mark to tell him I was rooting for him in the fight. I need his phone number."

I was taken aback. "*You* call him?"

"I can call him if I want to."

"Do you think *I* should call him too?" I asked eagerly.

"I'm sure you will regardless of what I say."

"What's that supposed to mean?"

"You're obsessed with Mark. You're the one who got him into this mess in the first place."

"How dare you!"

"It's so obvious that you're in love with him, I'm surprised you haven't gotten beat up sooner."

"For your information, I kicked Brett's ass! Not like you, crying on the floor."

"There were three of them!" James cried in his own defense.

"And second of all, I *don't* love Mark."

James didn't respond.

"Say something!" I said.

James said nothing at first, as if he was preparing an answer. "You're my best friend," he finally said, "I just want you to stop being such a creep."

"Yeah, well, you're *not* my best friend."

"*Fine!*" James hung up on me.

Neither of us actually had the courage to call Mark, so it was a surprise to both of us when Mark didn't come to school the next day. No one knew where he was. Meanwhile, the rumor that Mark was a faggot began to flourish. Anna claimed that Mark didn't seem interested in the "usual" things couples did, admitting that she'd wondered about him all along. Kevin told everyone that Mark had once grabbed his butt. I pictured him grabbing my butt and had to walk around positioning my Trapper Keeper carefully over my crotch so no one would realize the real faggot was me.

By the night of the championship game Mark still had not returned to school. Coach Pooch was livid, calling this "Mark's betrayal." Brett was appointed the new center and lost the ball on the first toss-up. The game only went downhill from there. Our team couldn't hang on to the ball to save our lives. It wasn't a game; it was a public humiliation. My only relief was that because Coach Pooch didn't dare let me in the game, no one could blame me when we lost the championship.

Coach Pooch was so upset afterward that I thought he was going to punch a hole in the wall. He wasn't the only one to lay the blame on Mark missing the game. "It's all Mark's fault that we lost the championship," Brett complained.

"Fucking faggot," Kevin added.

I felt my stomach sinking as I listened to them tear Mark to shreds. No matter what, the harassment would never end. It seemed like there was no point left in fighting them.

The truth about Mark's whereabouts was shared at last the next day. "Class, I regret to inform you that we have lost one of our students," Sister Mary Kelly began. "Mark Saddle has transferred to another school and won't be returning to St. Mark's."

There was a flurry of whispers. Katy asked, "What school is he going to?"

"Trinity."

I couldn't believe this news. Trinity was known as the strictest Catholic school in the world. An all-boys school, mass was delivered in Latin, kids had to wear more formal uniforms that included ties and blazers, and if you didn't know calculus by the time you were twelve, they spanked you.

"Why do you think Mark had to transfer to Trinity?" James asked at lunch.

"'Cause he's cursed like us," I said.

"What do you mean? He's . . ."

"Gay?" I shrugged. "I don't know. Listen, I never told you this, but at the retreat someone asked if it was a sin to be gay. It wasn't me."

James's eyes widened. "Do you think it was Mark?"

"I don't know. It was asked anonymously."

And I really didn't know—at least not for sure. After all, Mark had been the captain of the basketball team, the most popular boy in school dating the most popular girl in school. How *could* he be gay? Boys like James and me were gay. We were unpopular with everyone, and girls never paid attention to us, except to mention that we were losers. Although I'd never met "a real gay person" before, I was pretty sure that every one of them was dreadful at sports.

Then again, I might as well find out for sure.

Chapter 14

I decided to call Mark. Only every time I thought of
it—and I thought of it constantly—I chickened out.
I was scared of his family, scared of what he might say to
me. Maybe he blamed me for his situation. As James had
pointed out, it was all my fault.

Finally after two weeks of questioning myself, I realized that Mark wasn't going to call me, so if I didn't call
him I'd never see him again. I called.

Mark's dad answered. "You're not one of those
troublemakers from St. Mark's, are you?"

For the first time in my life I was a fast thinker. "No, I go to Trinity."

"Who's calling?"

I couldn't think of a fake name, so I just said, "Andy Bobsees," and prayed. It worked.

"Hello?" Mark said.

"Hi! It's Andy."

"*Andy?*"

Suddenly there were shuffling sounds on the other end of the line, as if Mark was taking the phone into another room.

"I'm not allowed to talk to people from St. Mark's," he whispered.

"What happened? Why'd you leave?"

"The fight—what the fight was about," Mark answered. "So they sent me to an all-boys school. The dumbest move given the circumstances."

"I wish I could go there with you," I confessed, wanting to ask him on the spot if he had been the boy to ask the question at the retreat. But he hadn't said he was gay, just that his dad thought he was a fag and had made him change schools because of it. What if I came out and said, "I'm gay," but Mark said, "I'm not"? He might even hate me.

"Hey, you still listen to that Nirvana CD?" he asked.

"Yeah."

"I heard Kurt Cobain is bisexual."

There was a short pause. He had said this almost as

if it were a dare. As if he would say what I'd hoped all along he'd say, but I'd have to make the first move.

"I sometimes wonder if I'm like that," I volunteered, "Like Kurt Cobain."

More silence. "So do I," Mark admitted. "I think I'm like him, too. Maybe even more than that."

Just as I was about to say the word we'd danced around, Mark said, "Hey, I gotta go. My dad's sniffin' around."

He hung up before I could say good-bye.

* * *

At lunch the next day I told James, "I hate everyone at this school."

"Do you hate me?"

"You're the only person left here that I like."

"Really? Thanks for being my friend."

I was surprised to hear that. Usually James hated me—and who could blame him? The realization that no matter what happened James and I would forever be best friends pleased me. "Hey, we should start working on that comic book!"

"Okay!"

"Should I come over after school?"

"Yeah!"

With Mark gone now, I spent most of my time with James, working on our comic book at his house. At first, we just drew characters we imagined would be cool in a comic book. My characters tended to look human, like Superman and Wonder Woman, while James leaned toward aliens and mutants. Only these aliens and mutants were too "cute," which I pointed out.

"Do you think I'll look cute when I grow up?" James asked.

"Yeah. You just need to get taller and have a cooler haircut."

"So do you!"

"What's wrong with my hair?"

Our comic book was set on an alien planet called Markazoid. The first issue opens with a span of Markazoid, which has a lava and stone terrain. Cut to the interior. Tasha (named after James's cat) narrowly escapes the doomed fortress with a pink jewel by transporting it to Earth. On Earth she plants the pink jewel in the forest, then transports home.

Along comes a group of attractive teenage campers, including one named Mark. Mark finds the pink jewel while hiking through the forest alone. But because Tasha has ingeniously charmed the stone to return to her the moment someone touches it, Mark is transported to Markazoid, and when the Markazoidians learn his name, they realize he was sent to save their planet from destruction.

"It's perfect," James said. "But don't you think we

should change the name from Mark before we show anyone?"

"How about we make it Mark for now and change it later?"

"Okay."

James and I were best friends again, and I didn't care much which lunchroom table we sat at. Also, I figured if James and I could get our comic book published, we'd be so rich that if our parents wanted any of our money, they would have to let us go to whatever school we wished to attend.

"I hope we get published," James gushed.

"If we do, I'm going to Hollywood," I announced.

"Me, too."

* * *

With Mark gone, the harassment of James got even worse. One afternoon on my way to recess, I came across James with a "kick me" sign taped to his back, shouting, "Stop it, guys," as Brett, Kevin, and Mathew hopped in circles around him, kicking his butt.

"Leave him alone!" I shouted, running up to them.

"Oh, look at what we have here," Brett laughed. "James's boyfriend wants us to leave him alone."

The guys turned all their attention on me. I put up my fists self-defensively.

"Nobody move!" Mr. Preston shouted.

"He started it!" Brett said, pointing at me.

"Brett, I saw enough of the scuffle from down the hall to draw my own conclusions." Mr. Preston took the "kick me" sign off James's back and held it up to their faces.

Brett stammered but couldn't muster up an excuse.

"I'll expect to see you, Kevin, and Mathew waiting in my office in two minutes."

Mr. Preston looked like he might yell at James and me next but instead said only, "I'm glad to see you two are a team again," and left for his office.

I found out the next day how Mr. Preston had punished those guys. Not only did Brett, Kevin, and Mathew have to write a paper titled "Jesus and Tolerance," but they were also made to do dishes at lunch for an entire month.

Suckers!

Chapter 15

Just when I thought my life without Mark couldn't go on, James shared with me the best news I'd heard in weeks. Mark's family had reemerged at Sunday mass, and Mark was there with them. I realized this might be the perfect opportunity to see Mark. Unfortunately, my family never went to church together, and showing up by yourself is lame, so I asked James, "Hey, can I sleep over on Saturday night and go to church with you on Sunday?"

"My parents will say no."

"At least ask. You *have* to."

On Saturday I called James, "What did your parents say?"

"About what?"

"*Duh!* About me going to church with you guys?"

"Oh . . . they said no."

"Did you even ask them?"

"*Yes,*" James said defensively.

"No, you didn't."

"I did!"

"Swear to God?"

"Your mom said I didn't have to answer you when you asked me that."

"See! You're lying! You never asked them!"

James scowled. "That's because I already know they'll say no."

"Just ask."

"*Fine.* I'll call you later when they tell me no all over again."

Since James was hopeless when it came to confronting his mother, I made a backup plan. "Mom, can we go to church tomorrow?"

"Since when do you want to go to church?"

Of course I had to lie; if my family knew I loved Mark, they'd hate me. "I miss church on Sundays."

"Do I have to go?" Amy asked.

"I'm not going," Dad said.

"We're in Catholic school!" I cried. "We're supposed to go to church."

"I'll take you to church," Mom said. "But next Sunday. I already have plans with Aunt Barb tomorrow."

"I don't understand why we don't go to church," I grumbled. "It's sacrilege!"

"Keep your jets cool," Dad said. "Mom's gonna take you to church next Sunday, so if you want to pray tomorrow, pray in your bedroom."

"Yeah, right. I'll just go by myself instead," I said.

"Now *there's* an idea," Dad said, probably figuring I wouldn't do it. I'm sure they thought my excuse of missing church sounded fishy. I rolled my eyes at the thought of my weird family. What kid has to beg his parents to go to church? No wonder I always got detention. My parents were faithless.

I would have gone to church by myself the next day, but I overslept. I blame Nintendo. When I finally got out of bed, I listened to Nirvana. After a while I decided to bike to James's house to see if he was home yet and interrogate him about Mark.

James's dad answered the door.

"Is James home?" I asked.

"Yes. He's upstairs with Mark Saddle."

Mark Saddle? James was upstairs with Mark Saddle? My Mark Saddle?

The house was surprisingly calm. Usually, everyone was there making a racket. Everyone except for Mark Saddle! In fact, I was positive that Mark Saddle had never been to James's house in his life, and therefore it had to be a mistake that he was here now. But what if James's dad was right? Had they met up at church and decided to hang out? Why would they want to hang out at James's house? James's house was a nightmare. Of course, the attic was pretty secluded in case they needed a place to . . . Oh my God!

I hopped the stairs two at a time the rest of the way, and when I reached James's landing I stopped to listen at his door. At first I didn't hear anything. Then I heard what sounded like a moan. It could be anyone! I was scared to find out, but I couldn't walk back down those stairs without knowing. I pushed the door open slowly, and there they were, Mark and James, in James's bed, dressed only in underwear. All I could see was Mark's white briefs as he straddled James. "Oh my God!" I screamed and darted back down the stairs.

"Andy, wait!" Mark called after me.

* * *

I ran all the way from James's house to the triangle, which, at the beginning of the school year, was where the gang had played football. Now no one was there. I plopped down on the muddy grass hill, shivering from the cold but refusing to budge. I knew what I had seen, because I had played that game with James dozens of times. I wanted to kill James. How could he have betrayed me like this? He'd gone behind my back and stolen Mark from me. I wanted to kill Mark. I felt so powerless and all alone that I sobbed to myself in despair. Did this happen to other gay kids? Was I not good enough for James and Mark? Would I ever find someone to love me?

Please, God, guide me in my time of need. I swear I'm a faithful Catholic in spite of my family. All I really want is to be happy. . . . I want to find someone who loves me as much as I love him. Thank you for all the gifts you've given me.

After my prayer I finally decided to go home. Three blocks away, I remembered that I had left my bike at James's house. I decided to go back and sneak my bike away without anyone seeing me.

When I arrived, I found James and Mark sitting on the front porch, fully clothed. All three of us froze. Both Mark and James stared at me, looking like they expected me to breathe fire. But as much as I hated what they'd done, as much as I wanted revenge, I couldn't bring myself to really hate them. Not in the way I hated Brett or Anna. They'd gone behind my back, and I wasn't ready to forgive or forget that. Still, these were my friends, the only real friends I ever had. Without them, there was no one. Mark and James were like me, and something about seeing them together on the front porch made me feel left out. So I decided to join them.

We walked toward nowhere in particular, all of us silent the whole time. Mark and James were a few steps ahead of me. I couldn't guess what they were thinking. I couldn't stand the suspense any longer. "Are you two, like, boyfriends together?"

"We're just friends," Mark said. "Like me and you. Like you and James."

We walked all the way to the Mississippi River and climbed down the bank. At the river's edge we sat on a fallen tree.

"Don't worry, Andy. What happened changes nothing. The three of us will always be friends," Mark said, putting his arm around me.

I thought about that and realized that I so wanted both of them as my friends. "Thanks, guys," I said.

"So, now what?" James asked.

"I dunno," Mark said.

We sat there quietly for a moment. Then I asked Mark and James if they had heard the Mississippi River was pumped full of so much sewage that a certain worm had mutated, and some kids who thought it was safe to swim had come out of the water with worms in their ears. Eventually the worms killed them, but not before they'd gone insane and killed everyone in their school.

They loved my story.

* * *

That night I sat in my bedroom, listening to Nirvana. The thought of Mark and James made me grin. Those silly faggots! I went to my mirror and stared at my reflection. "Congratulations, Beverly," I said to myself, "you made it on your own."

I pulled my drawings of Mark out from under my toy box and looked through them. I thought about destroying them, since I didn't need them anymore—I wasn't living in that fantasy world—but on second thought put them back. I found a red crayon and decided to admit something in writing that I'd always expected to take to my grave up until that day. On the wall behind my dresser I wrote in big, thick letters:

I AM GAY.

Special thanks for Don Weise,
whose wisdom is my guiding light;
Michael Mancilla, who acts like
my big brother and my big sister;
and Dan Freeman, whose love
inspired me to look back on my
wonder years fondly.